# THINGS

2015

M.G. ALLEN

Cover art: Arthur Asa
Cover Design: George Cotronis
Editor: Lori Michelle
Interior Design: Lori Michelle

ISBN: 978-91-979725-3-6

www.krakenpress.com

# CHAPTER 1

WATCHING HIS POTENTIAL landlord step out of his beat-up truck, Jason thought: *It would be nice if I could rent an apartment from someone who would spruce things up once in a while.*

His previous landlord used to collect the rent barefoot in a dirty Scooby-Doo bathrobe, reeking of a smell best described as cat litter and Cheetos. His name was Bruce. Before that was Shelly. She was middle-aged with a really bad perm, hobbling around the complex in butt ugly pantsuits and florescent flip-flops. She smelled like bug spray.

Mike Shibble had long dried mustard stains down the front of his t-shirt, along with blotches of something else, ratty jeans, disheveled hair and an unkempt beard that resembled a frightened Brillo pad. He had childish little hands and bulging bowling pin forearms covered with curly blond hairs.

While giving him a tour of the inside, Mike took a special interest in showing him the laundry room.

"See that window over the washing machine?" He said extending a pudgy finger. "Keep it shut."

"Why?"

"Something might get in from the outside."

Jason pointed at the window that was already open.

It was a small rectangular window, glass on the inside, and a screen on the outside that was sloppily taped up. The window was halfway open on its track.

The landlord shot him an angry glance.

"Don't shut it all the way either."

"Why not?"

"Something might break it trying to get in."

"Something?"

"Well, you know . . . "

"Bums? Tigers? What?"

The place was decent enough for Jason's standards. It was clean with a nice new kitchen sink, no bad smells, no stains on the carpet. The doors and cabinets didn't wobble on the hinges. Mike took pride in pointing out that the cabinets were brand new. They had a nice fresh wood smell to them. The landlord might not have been a Renaissance man but he looked like he was skilled with tools.

The paint job inside wasn't spectacular. The beige walls were a little dirt smudged and had some divots in them. The sheetrock wasn't in the best of shape.

When the summertime came, it would be murder: not much circulation. The window air conditioner unit looked like it hadn't been serviced in a long time, and was thickly clotted with dust. This wasn't a huge deal, but Jason had to factor it in.

It was cheap. That was a plus. Only 400 bucks a month. Not too bad despite the trash-strewn lawn and rusty refrigerator embedded in the front yard.

"It's raccoons," Mike explained in a not-too-confident voice. "We got raccoons that like to hang out in that alley behind the building. We're trying to get rid of them. Dang animal services are being a bunch of lazy butts."

He chuckled in a forced way that spoke: *You believe me, right*?

"That's strange behavior for raccoons." Jason remarked. "They like to sneak inside of the washing machine? I guess that would explain where the missing socks go."

Mike didn't appreciate this attempt at humor, furrowing his brows. "Don't do your laundry at night. Keep the washing machine lid down. In fact, how about just staying out of the laundry room altogether? There's a coin laundry a few blocks away. Use that."

Jason was not a fan of coin laundry: thick detergent filled air, that drab flump-flump-flump of dryers spinning, the over-filled trash cans, dirty kids running around. A laundromat was such a depressing place; a depot for sad lonely looking people on that all-too-familiar human hamster wheel of washing-drying-folding, washing-drying-folding, washing-drying-folding . . .

It was the perfect microcosm metaphor of life though: wash-dry-fold, wash-dry-fold. In between the time you read a few magazine articles, listen to a few tunes on your headphones, then die.

In the end, a bargain was a bargain. The place, although a bit seedy looking, was reasonably close to Jason's job and very close to his favorite diner. There was also a decent Chinese restaurant around the corner, Willie Chan's.

Willie Chan's had a reputation for being the least authentic Chinese restaurant in town. The Food & Drink section of the newspaper might deplore such a place but to Jason, it was perfect.

He had three criterions for an authentic Chinese restaurant: Did it have orange sauce? Did it give you rice in a cardboard container with a little metal handle? Did it have red lanterns hanging inside?

If yes, it was an authentic Chinese restaurant.

His former roommate, Carlos, was giving him until the end of the month to get out. Carlos was on a big power trip. He wanted to turn Jason's room into his personal studio for his lousy "paintings", justifying his lack of proper notice by pointing out trivial things Jason wasn't doing around the house: a few dirty dishes, a wayward t-shirt on the sofa, a sock in the hallway . . .

Carlos had consistently been a tyrant for the last five months, wielding his lease holding status like some power mad child-king.

Jason couldn't stand the guy. Jason usually went to the all-night diner to avoid having to face him. Carlos liked to paint in the den, blocking the TV, blasting his 80's Brit pop bands.

Most of Jason's roommate situations ended up like this; petty territorial disputes, ridiculous arguments, silly one-upmanships. It didn't matter how great of friends they started out being, cohabitating would kill it. Someone could save you from drowning, pull you from a burning house, or rescue you from a man-eating tiger, but after living with them for eight months, all respect is lost.

Just a few farts, dirty dishes, and unflushed toilets could do that.

Hell was other people. Good call, Mr. Sartre.

Carlos did that shit on purpose. He had the bigger room. His easel fit into it perfectly with room to spare.

He *had* to use the living room.

He would lay all of his paints and brushes generously around the room so that coming in through the door was an obstacle course, shitty eighties pop music surging through the sheetrock giving Jason no quarter, no escape.

Then . . . off to the diner with a book in hand and never in a good mood.

Sometimes the diner was fun. Diners were good for reading, coffee drinking and weirdo watching. Strippers and hookers with stretch marks, smeared make-up and disheveled hair, sipping coffee and munching greasy food. He'd see large groups of college kids fraternizing and late night club goers dressed all too nicely for such a place, wearing bling-bling galore.

Lately, the most intriguing person at the diner was a guy who wore a long black suit with bright pink lapels, a rose in his pocket, black slacks, dress shoes and a top hat. He looked like a magician. Sitting in the corner booth reading, Jason kept expecting the guy to whisk towards him and start pulling long scarves out of his sleeves. Or remove the top hat and procure a rabbit, transform the napkin dispenser into a dove.

But the strangely dressed dude just sat there with his coffee, staring out the plate glass window into the dreary night.

Jason's current theory was that the guy was an unemployed magician. Maybe he lost his job at the club due to excessive drinking. Maybe he suited up into his magician outfit just to fool his wife that he was still employed, but came to the diner to drown his sorrows in bitter black coffee while contemplating his next career move. *I should've been a floor tile salesman like my dad,* he was probably thinking. *God, I'm such a loser. Maybe I'll go to bartender school. I'd be a good bartender. I could even work some of my magician skills in while serving drinks . . .*

Jason got so bored sitting there some nights he had created an entire imaginary life for the guy, complete with a wife who collected TV Guides and had them indexed under the coffee table.

Jason saw cute girls there sometimes. He was currently scoping a doll-faced night waitress who already told him she had a boyfriend. Maybe he could wait it out . . .

No Jill replacement yet. He and Jill had broken up three months ago, just six months after he left college. Jill was Ms. Perfect: cute with short blond hair, and smart, worldly-wise. He met her in English 102. She was the only girl he had ever met, and would ever meet, who owned most of Philip K. Dick's books.

More even than he'd read. It seemed impossible.

She liked to drink a little, party a little, but never too much. That was impressive for a girl, a girl that can go out and kick up her heels then still stay home and read other times, a girl that could talk about Edgar Allan Poe, Flannery O'Conner, and John Waters movies in the same conversation.

She was a good balance between highbrow and low brow, just like him.

Leaving college and working retail had been the

beginning of the end. Her calls were less and less frequent. Throughout his basically crappy year, he'd been holding onto hope that they could get back together. That hope was diminishing now like the summer in late August.

Maybe his new apartment would unleash some new possibilities.

God knows he could use some.

***

He signed the lease the next day and handed over the security deposit. He had barely enough money. Jason was worried about the credit check. What the hell is a credit check? When did this start? He never even had a credit card. His school loans might have been a problem, since he was well in arrears.

Nothing happened.

Mike Shibble called him at his job that day and informed him that everything was all right. He had to call Jason's job and Carlos as well, for references. Smooth sailing there.

At last, the day arrived, the first of October, emancipation from Carlos, and a new apartment.

He had no furniture. A sofa was a dream at this point. The old sofa belonged to Carlos. It was an ugly beige piece of junk anyway. He would be sofa-less for now. He did have a futon bed; it was a pain in the ass to haul. He had to bug the shit out of Dave to borrow his roommate's truck to haul it over.

Of course, furniture was a purely subjective term. He found a few folding lawn chairs a block away on the trash curb in decent condition. The seats looked pretty worn out but he planned to reinforce them with some duct tape. Being single, desperate, and poor made a man quite creative. A fresh trash curb offered a wealth of opportunity, the proverbial El Dorado, to a retail wage slave like himself.

Cooking supplies were a different story. He was in dire need of kitchen things, but decided to pick them up piecemeal as soon as his finances recovered from the two hundred dollar security deposit. His bi-monthly paycheck couldn't come soon enough.

Luckily he stole Carlos's can opener, a spoon, knife and three forks. He had no illusions that Carlos wouldn't know he took it.

He'd deny it. Just to drive Carlos crazy.

The first week in his new place was wonderful and peaceful. It was his first apartment all to himself, a personal milestone indeed. Instead of staring bleary-eyed out of a diner window, he sat inside his own place with a few Budweiser cans in a trash-picked lawn chair, plucking the guitar. Maybe he would finally excel on the guitar beyond three chords.

He hadn't met any of the other neighbors. He was laying low for the time being. So far, he had seen a Goth-looking chick coming and going, her Dr. Martins clumping down the wooden stairs at odd times.

He heard some loud music blasting two doors down, punctuated by assorted yelps, grunts, and expletives. Young, dumb and loud types. These were folks to avoid.

Surely, there had to be some adults or near-adults inhabiting the place, but that didn't matter yet.

Friends could be made later. Getting settled was priority number one.

***

His tranquility was punctured as soon as he realized he had no more clean underwear or socks. He had procrastinated as long as possible, worn the same pair of underwear three days straight; socks, four. There had to be some cosmic retribution for doing that.

*Face it. You've got a date with that coin laundry tonight,* said that voice in his head, as he re-alphabetized the science fiction section at work. He was gloomy all day about it.

Before work he had ducked into the coin laundry, just to acclimate himself with his doom. A fat homeless guy was sleeping on the floor on a bed of newspapers. A corkboard bulletin board was on the wall advertising someone's thrash metal band, a missing dog and, strangely, a faded photograph of a penis.

By the time he returned home that night, determined to grab his sack of laundry and take his medicine, he found himself devoid of the will to face that depressing shithole of a laundromat.

How ridiculous was it that there was only one laundromat on this side of town? It was like people without their own washing machines were lepers.

*Sorry, Mr. S. Your no laundry at night rule has got to go down.*

What kind of rule was that anyway? Who'd ever heard of night laundry being hazardous? Mr. Shibble was just trying to be a mini-despot like all landlords, keeping their tenant kingdom down with an iron fist.

Besides, he still had half a box of detergent leftover from his last apartment. This was another indicator of Carlos's miserly ways: buy your own detergent. Carlos didn't like him using the lavender scented stuff he bought in the fancy aisle of the supermarket.

The dude spent fifteen bucks for that shit. What a chump.

So he did it. He washed his laundry that night.

Let the raccoons come.

While he was separating, he dared to lean close to the window. A stinky odor wafted in on a gust of fall wind.

*There must be a garbage heap down there*, he thought.

He awoke later to hear a crash from the laundry room, glass breaking, metal bending. Something was trying to get into the window.

*That's one enormous raccoon if it was one.* It would have to be a raccoon on steroids; a super-raccoon.

It would also have to be able to climb a wall. The window was too high from the ground for a raccoon, without standing on the shoulders of five other raccoons. It finally hit Jason how far-fetched Mr. Shibble's explanation had been.

He didn't investigate until the morning. The window was cracked; the frame bent like it was pulled from the outside. A dank smell filled the room.

Dirt and grass follicles were streaked on part of the wall, across the dryer and washer. He spotted some kind of greenish blue oily substance among the muddy sludge.

He was pretty shaken up all day. Luckily the store wasn't too busy, allowing him some peace. He got to stock magazines, which was a plus. He could check out the latest issues and gawk the boobies on the men's magazines.

Roger wasn't there. Janet was the manager on duty. Janet was the cool manager, not overly uptight like most and certainly not a snooty whip-cracker like Roger.

A Chris Issacs album crooned over his head as he restocked his section. After that came Celine Dion. Apparently that musical abomination was still in the recording business.

The music the Book Barn played was always lousy. There had to be some kind of OSHA law against it, some legislation to protect workers from shrilly vocals, canned instrumentation, and piss-poor perfunctory lyrics. Pop music was so notorious for that, always striving to manipulate human emotions in the worst possible ways, dangling carrots of lost love, the need for acceptance, alienation, greed, sex, outrage . . .

Every musical genre from pop to metal, from country to hip-hop had some kind of pathetic human emotion it was trying to trigger. For that all-important reason, of course: money money money!

One funny thing: Carlos sent him a text message on his phone. The jig was up.

"I KNOW U STOLE THE CAN OPENER MOTHERFUCHER."

*Come and get it, motherfucher.*

Jason planned to text back later, maybe tomorrow. Play dumb on the issue. Keep this going until Carlos gives up.

Compared to Jason, Carlos' income was bourgeois. He could afford a can opener without putting a huge dent in his food budget.

That night, Jason kept the blinds open on the front window, hoping to see another tenant outside. Then he would pop out there and ask them what was back in the alley. If he didn't see anyone he would just go to the Goth girl's door, knock and ask her. Take a gamble.

Besides, she was fairly cute. Usually girls who go overboard with the Goth thing intimidated him. He was feeling adventurous these days.

He was torn. He had been talking to his ex earlier, which had stirred up emotions. She didn't mention seeing anyone at the moment but the suspicion remained. It was eating at him. He knew there would be some horndog jerk sniffing around her at that college, some hoity-toity slickster calling her up, working the angles to draw her in.

Guys were so like that, especially rich college kids with nothing to do but hang around campus and party.

Those bastards.

His better judgment won out. Play it cool. Don't bother the Goth chick.

She was a girl that lived alone and most likely wouldn't appreciate strangers knocking on her door asking her about creatures sneaking into the window.

That wouldn't be good at all.

***

He discovered another tenant; an older woman getting into her car. She was tastefully dressed with small oval glasses and a short frumpy physique. She struck him as the most perfect person to ask. She couldn't accuse him of hitting on her. She had a calm, breezy look about her that told him she was mature and seasoned enough not to freak out.

He decided to bide his time. He had to go about this carefully to not seem like a nutcase. Or seem like a frequent drug user hallucinating monsters.

Did other people have raccoons sneaking into their place, if so, how severe? It would help if he could see what the alley looked like. It was just a small space between his building and the boarded up one behind it.

A high ratty fence shut off both ends of it, loops of barb wire along the top. Usually this was to keep derelicts from camping out, he knew. It was strange that the barb wire portion at the top was bent towards the inside, like it was meant to keep something *in.*

He had meant for it to be a quiet night, planning on devouring part of the James Ellroy novel that he had borrowed from work, part of the library-like check out system there. He would buy it anyway, when it came out in paperback.

A techno blast from his cell phone called out to him from the floor. He hated the ring setting but had yet to reset it. He was still trying to figure that stupid cell phone.

Big Bad Dave was on the line. He asked Jason how his new apartment was going. Of course Jason knew the long-and-short of it was “Let’s go out for beers”. Some co-workers had tried to pull him out for drinks also, to some ritzy joint in mid-town. Party fever seemed to be in the air. He was resisting it well though.

He felt guilty after hitting up Dave for the truck so he couldn’t say no.

They were going to meet up at the Urban Turban, the place they always went. It had been almost two weeks since he’d been there, since he’d been sorting his apartment business out. As bored as he was getting with the Turban, it was still crucial to keep his faltering social life alive.

It was the trendiest of the trendy places right now. It could be worse he supposed. Pseudo-hipsters were the least hated on his Most Hated Personality Type list. Two-faced corporate types like Roger were at the very top, sharing the coveted space with jocks and policemen.

Hipsters were pretty harmless. They were near the

bottom of the list, with religious whackos and Techno Club jerks. Hell, he probably fit the mold as a hipster himself. Everybody has some kind of category these days, filed and indexed by their work, marriage statuses, entertainment choices, clothing style, hairstyle . . . it's the world we live in.

If he entered all the important information about his current life in a huge marketing computer, pressed enter, a little slip of paper would come out saying HIPSTER.

So be it then.

"You can't make a living being a hipster," his dad had said to him once. In fact that was when he first time he considered his relationship to the term.

Things could be worse. It was the most amorphous personality type so he didn't have to feel confined.

All the drunk and silly twenty-somethings at the Urban Turban could slip passed this label because they were taking classes and taking exams. They appeared normal, doing something with their lives.

Maybe he was just jealous. They were just college kids partying, enjoying their youths. Why shouldn't they? They had futures. He had been one of them once, before he took on too many college loans and dropped out. The student loans were a different story all together.

At least the music was pretty good and beers were cheap: one dollar Pabst Blue Ribbon pint cans and little bowls of pretzels.

The Turban was unique because it was underground, a club built from a renovated parking garage. It had different sections, a maze of little nooks, some lit up with strobes and colors, some with candles in glass jars.

It had a dance floor, lounge and a live band area. Jason preferred the lounge area but was often dragged out to the dancing area, although they just sat there and didn't dance, but watched. Most of the girls were out there. Jason, on principle, didn't try to pick women up in bars.

It was too much work. Working was what he did in the daytime. At night, he liked to sit.

Dave liked to work on the girls sometimes. He was pretty good at it, could turn it on and off like a switch, an admirable quality in the eyes of a wallflower like Jason.

He and Jason went to college together and both dropped out about the same time. They met in a Psych 101 class. Dave had a lazy, smart-ass sense of humor like Jason, and had a pointed disdain for the simple-minded twits in society. He was a reader but didn't act standoffish and superior.

Jill once said they had a bro-mance. "A text-book example bromance," were her exact words. That was a funny term. It wasn't quite a bro-mance, he told her, because neither were the bromantic types.

Dave was currently a shoe salesman at a suburban mall. Chris came out to the club with them too, another college friend, except he was still attending school. His major was undeclared but was considering a science degree.

They were the main three. Other people they knew sometimes dropped by, cramming into the fake leather booth in the corner of what Urban Turban liked to refer to as the "ballroom".

That night, their conversation started out on the subject of nicknames, and guys who gave themselves nicknames. The bar back was named Lotus. He had given himself that name. He bounced around The Turban, cleaning, grabbing glasses, empties, trash, and hitting on girls when he could. He was also a bassist in a mediocre band.

"Every time somebody gives themselves a nickname, it's lame as hell. Why is that?" asked Dave.

"Because nicknames are fucking stupid," said Chris, as if this was patently obvious, as he pulled on a cigarette.

"I refuse to believe it's that simple, Chris."

"You have to earn a nickname," explained Jason. "Giving yourself a nickname is stupid because you're trying too hard to create an image for yourself."

"True."

"Your friends have to give you a nickname or it's bogus.

Your cellmates or fellow gang members can give you a nickname because you're some sort of hardcore dude. You've got to earn it. "

"If Lotus wants to be Lotus, let him, right?" said Dave. "He tries too hard though."

"It reeks of desperation."

"Like a landfill in mid-August."

"Did you check out his new tattoos? All the way up to his wrists."

"Barbed wire. That's so hard core."

"Tattoos." said Chris. "I'll never understand the fascination with those things."

"And piercings!"

"When'll it all end?" said Chris. "My sister's got a big dragon tattoo down her back and she's an elementary school teacher!"

"Even soccer moms get tattoos. The edgy mystique of tattoos, needless to say, has run its course."

"It baffles the mind. People think it's so rebellious to ink pictures into their skin. What's so rebellious about doing something everyone else is doing?"

"They're expensive, too." said Chris. "I wish I had that kind of dough to skank myself up with!"

"Shame on us, squandering our money on food and shelter. Lotus probably lives with a girl or with his mom."

"I think he lives with a girl. He's got that carefree look about him that says he gets laid all the time."

"Grrrrrr!"

"More power to him."

Dave raised his beer can and they clinked.

Lotus came by and scooped up their empties into a huge tub. Dave started a bit of conversation with him, making friendly small-talk, asking about his band. Jason couldn't hear any of it, due to the thundering music. The real content of conversations never mattered in a place like the Turban. With the decibel level and the constant swirl of colored lights, deep insightful conversations were discouraged, in the ballroom anyway. The lounge was a better place for that.

Jason joked with Chris, talking about some of the characters they had known when he was going to college and some freaky parties they had gone to. They watched the crowds of people bounce by. The place was filling up. It always filled up.

Usually, he was fighting depression in this place, but now, he was a tad upbeat being out of Carlos's yoke. He had to have fun tonight. He would force himself.

He chugged another Pabst pint can quickly, letting the alcohol spike his mood. He felt himself becoming more animated, dominating the conversation with Chris, something he usually didn't do. He tried to crack a joke with a girl who was waiting for her drink, but she didn't hear him and kept asking, "What?" over and over until he was too exasperated to repeat himself again.

In the back of his mind, Jill kept creeping up. As soon as he tried to bring up the subject with Chris, the evening revelry began to nosedive. He went into his former relationship too deeply and started sounding like a maudlin dork. Too many couples and slick player-types around made him feel lonely. Dave started chatting up some girl making Jason feel weak and inferior.

Eventually, Chris ran into another friend, then another group of friends, and was swallowed up in the lights and noise, leaving Jason propped up against the bar wondering what the fuck he was supposed to do to justify being there. Already nursing his fourth Pabst, he was dangerously close to becoming a drunken basket case, staggering around the club, eyeballing everyone, garbling his words.

He whipped out his cell phone and pretended to check it, playing Minesweeper until he got a second wind and broke out of his trance. Sometimes he could be inspired to joke more with strangers; maybe meet somebody new, somebody with something interesting to talk about.

In the course of the next hour, a Pabst-soaked fog of an hour, he spotted two girls whom he almost mistook for Jill, below average height cuties with short blond hair. The last girl he tapped on the shoulder. She sneered at him. Her hair wasn't even blond. It was red.

Lately, it was like some ultra-powerful form of horniness had possessed him. He had a very strange dream the night before involving his fifth grade Social Studies teacher, Ms. Morgan. She had been voluptuous as he remembered her, but in his dream she was wearing a negligee and garter belts, holding a can of Reddi-Whip.

It was one of those kinds of dreams normal people were embarrassed to admit to having.

He wondered if his current horny state was normal. Horniness was just powerful like that, he figured, rearing its head, in huge waves that always seemed to be at some pinnacle, some overwhelming do-or-die state. Evolutionary trickery whose end product was laughably predictable.

He knew then it was time to scat the Turban. He elbowed Dave who was now sitting on the same side of the booth with the girl, his arm around her. The guy was good.

Jason lied, said he had to get up early the next day. Dave gave him a thumb's up.

As he was heading out the door, he saw The Magician sitting at the door, looking as he had in the diner, brooding and alone but instead of a coffee mug, he had a plastic cup with some sort of drink, and a lime wedge floating in it.

Jason nodded in greeting at him, but the poor guy didn't respond.

At least Jason could take heart in the fact that he wasn't the most pathetic person at the bar.

# CHAPTER 2

THAT NIGHT, ABOUT ten thirty, he heard motion in the laundry room again. He thought his mind was playing tricks on him at first.

Metal bending, bits of glass tinkling on the floor.

He waited. He put down his James Ellroy novel and turned down the sound on his CD player, listening. Were the neighbors complaining about his noise? Did they drop something?

The noise distinctly came from the back room, the laundry room.

Beyond the chipped yellow door came a creak here, a creak there . . . the sound of the washing machine tilting and rocking not forcefully but with considerable strength.

Didn't raccoons make cute chirping sounds?

Then a bang. Ten seconds later there was another bang. Then another.

A loud one.

The thing in there was trying to open the washing machine lid.

A few more bangs separated by intense seconds.

Then dead silence.

Before approaching the laundry room door, he got the plunger from the bathroom. It was the only thing resembling a weapon he possessed.

He opened the door slowly, just a bit at a time until he was sure something wouldn't jump up and attack him. When he had the door halfway open, he shoved it open all the way, plunger extended chest high.

At first, he thought it was a snake. An enormous greenish blue tail hung down the side of the washing machine. His heart palpitated. Goosebumps arose. An inclination came to him that maybe he should hit it, kill it.

*Be a man. Hit that fucking thing.*

It was awfully big though.

*Are you going to be able to sleep tonight with that big monster hanging out of your washing machine?*

He wasn't sure how long it really was. Maybe it was twice that size. Half of it, maybe more, was curling inside the washing unit.

Good Lord. Was it an anaconda? Could an anaconda exist in this part of the world?

It wasn't scaly like a snake.

Nope, more like a slug. Its body was slick and wet, like gelatin, flattening against the white metal of the machine. Its color was hard to determine; a greenish-blue that darkened and lightened with its delicate undulations.

It was rising, peeling itself from the machine, moving so slow a minute or two passed before Jason realized it was reacting to his presence. A yellowish orb emerged from the tail as it dangled in mid-air.

It was looking at him.

"Hello," said Jason.

The creature didn't move. Albeit weird and mulch-smelling, it seemed to be a peaceful creature.

*Leave it alone. If it wants to burrow in the washing machine, let it.*

Hopefully it would do its business and go. No biggie.

Slugs were pretty harmless anyway, right? They were nice, ecologically friendly animals. They ate leaves and grass.

No wait. He remembered: They ate dead things.

*Dead things.*

There was a knock on his front door. He answered it.

An old woman stood there, shoulder-length white hair and small glasses. The other tenant, the other grown-up type besides himself.

"Hi, my name is Sandra Millman. I live in room 3 downstairs."

Jason introduced himself as well.

"I teach art at Georgia Perimeter some miles away. I'm probably the oldest tenant here, not just age-wise. I've been here for about, um, fifteen years now, I think."

She paused, smiled.

"I'm not trying to tell you my life story. Sorry. Perhaps you have other things to do right now?"

"No. Yeah, maybe. Sort of. Just don't pull any Jehovah's Witness stuff on me."

She laughed.

*Nice levity. Get her out of your door quick but don't make it too obvious.*

"It's fine. Really."

He gave her some tidbits of his own life, where he worked . . . yadda yadda. Ms. Millman finally got down to brass tacks.

"Did something try to get into your back window last night?"

"Yeah, actually. I think I did hear something."

"Figures. You and I are the only ones whose windows aren't boarded up from the outside. Of course Mike didn't properly warn you. He's just a greedy old slumlord anyway. Only three people live here so he's just trying to milk whatever profits he can from this wretched old unit before it's eventually condemned. Those slug monsters kept trying to get into my washer. I dumped salt all over my floor."

She smiled proudly.

"That kept them out. I found some greenish blue globules on the floor that morning, you can bet. They haven't bothered me since. You should do the same."

"Sure, if I see some. Slug monsters? Wow."

*Clever diversion!*

"I didn't really mean to say monsters, like they are dangerous. They're totally harmless, nice even. Don't be afraid of them."

"No. I can handle them," Jason said.

Her little white head darted into his door then out.

"Mind if I take a look in your laundry room?"

"Um . . . "

"I'll make it quick," Sandra said.

"Sorry. No time right now. I'm heading out to meet some friends," he lied. "Thanks for the advice though. I'll do that salt thing."

"Please try to capture one if you can. We need to find out how safe these things are."

"Capture one?" Jason raised an eyebrow.

"In a cage or something."

"In a cage?"

"Nevermind. Look, I'm not going to bullshit you anymore."

She handed him a card. It had been in her hand the whole time. He took it.

"Here's my number. If one comes into your apartment, call me. This could be some kind of new rare species that could benefit us. I've got the right contacts all lined up. I know some people at the science department at my school and they know some people. If some kind of profit comes from this we'll split it. Just make sure you keep silent about this in regards to Mike Shibble. He could ruin the whole thing. Mum's the word."

"Okay."

"On second thought, don't even try to capture it. Call me and I'll help you. We got a deal?"

She held out her hand. He shook it.

"Deal."

She adjusted her purse strap.

"I need to get moving inside. Please call me if you get a visit. Thanks, Jason."

"No, thank *you*."

She turned away.

Back in the laundry room, the slug creature was the same. The tail perked up again when it saw Jason, a languid motion like a lazy wave. The glassy yellow eye opened up. It was not quite yellow, after all. It was gold, a shimmering golden eye.

As it raised itself up, the tip formed a circle. It didn't look like some random motion a cat would make with its tail because the circle left the yellow eye at the top.

Like a face.

The eye blinked.

Slowly the tail uncurled from its circle then made it again. The eye blinked.

Then again and then again.

Meanwhile the rest of its body went about its business within the bowels of the washer, the inner mechanisms quietly creaking and groaning.

It was trying to communicate. Without deliberation, Jason made a circle with his own fingers and thumb, sort of like the A-Okay symbol without the other three fingers sticking up.

The tail rose up and down in slow gentle motions, like it was nodding. Then it relaxed and drooped lazily down the side of the washer. Colors undulated within its strange skin.

Sleeping? Feasting on goodies from the lint trap? It was anyone's guess. Whatever it was doing, Jason just gave it permission to keep on doing it.

This was no garden variety slug. It was an intelligent one.

Jason put on his shoes and whipped up his coat. He put a novel into his backpack.

It was just like old times. He was heading to the diner.

***

He arrived back a few hours later, bleary-eyed, and didn't peek into the laundry room.

Tomorrow. He'd check up with it tomorrow.

From the diner, he used his cell phone to trade days with

one of his co-workers so he could have the next day off. Robert whined about it. Jason bargained with him. He offered comic books but Robert didn't bite. He offered to get him a bag of weed although Jason had shunned this habit for over a year now.

So had Robert.

At last, Jason offered to buy him beers at the Turban for a month, Pabsts only. No expensive imports. Robert caved. He'd work for Jason the next day.

The stage was set. He would get to the bottom of this slug business.

He suspected the old lady was fooling with him. It was probably her creature, her pet, some bizarre breed of snake. She gave him her card so he wouldn't complain to Mike. Jason entertained the idea that she was some kind of rare animal smuggler who had lost the thing and was trying to keep it under wraps.

*How stupid does she think I am?* Sprinkle salt on the floor? Catch it in a cage? She obviously took him for a dim-wit.

She was not to be trusted.

***

The next morning he discovered an entire litter of slug creatures writhing within the tub and agitator inside the washer. Strange wet sounds perked up his ears as he was loading the coffee machine.

They crawled in and out of each other, a big gooey, slimy squirming mass; their oily blue-green color catching the morning sunlight along their backs creating a glowing effect. Even weirder, they reacted to his presence like Big Mama, tiny worm heads flicked up in his direction.

Big Mama was gone. Maybe forever.

Peering out of the window, he saw a dark smudge on the concrete below. Perhaps it was a giant dried puddle of slug urine. Maybe it was just any old stain on concrete, un-slug related. Maybe it was Big Mama's body, dead and dissolving in the sun.

He still didn't know what to do with them. He wasn't going to call Ms. Millman. He trusted Big Mama more than he did her. He couldn't subject these newborn . . . whatevers . . . to some hideous laboratory. Big Mama wouldn't approve.

*You don't want to piss off something that size.*

Besides, they were interesting to him at the moment. A new apartment, new neighbors, and a dead-in-the-water love life spurred him to find some intermittent curiosity to peg his boredom to. Pretty soon, an unmarked van would pull up; people in sunglasses would knock on his door and whisk the critters away back to whatever lab created them.

Having the day off, he called a few people. Dave gave him the low down on his little pick-up; no sexual escapades to report. He overdid it. The girl seemed a little put off by his slick maneuvers. She left with her friends later that night. Jason offered condolences.

Next, he called Jill. He hadn't called her in over a week.

Both of them congratulated him on his new apartment. They promised some kind of house warming party. He discouraged this. No social butterfly, he. They were well aware.

"This shithole would just depress you," he told Dave. "If you insist on some kind of Jason's-got-a-new-apartment fanfare, just pop over with some PBRs and roach motels. You don't even have to gift wrap them."

He told Dave he'd meet him for beers at the Urban Turban that Friday, if he had the money. He told Jill they should meet up for coffee in the next few weeks, after her finals.

At the tail-end of his conversation with Dave, he saw something strange. It took him a while to even notice something different. Being late morning, the sun cast bright light into the room so it wasn't until the sun passed behind a cloud that he was able to zero in on the greenish blue plume hanging in the air.

It was no trick of light.

The plume made a circle, that familiar golden eye staring

at him, just a slit this time. The golden eye had a more ethereal look, flickering like some kind of winking God, stoic, wise and strange.

The circle gracefully unfurled, furled again, then again . . .

Jason made the finger circle thing.

The wise spirit nodded like before and started floating away. It drifted slowly and stopped. It cruised a little more almost rounding the corner to the kitchen, then paused again and stopped.

It just floated in the air, hovering, vibrating like a piece of tinsel among choppy winds. It made another kind of movement, one of its cryptic gestures. The one eye flickered. That bright beaming eye was becoming impatient.

He figured it out. It wanted him to follow it.

Jason followed.

It made a circle again but with a tail dangling like a sideways **P** over his kitchen counter.

Like a finger, a pointing finger now.

It took him several minutes to catch on. Then he realized it was pointing at the refrigerator door.

He opened it, and held the door while staring at the creature inquisitively. The swirling tendril swooped in, immediately encircling the paper container of orange chicken stir fry, his dinner from almost two weeks ago. Several other containers were behind it.

He laughed out loud. The strangeness of the encounter kept distracting him from completing the creature's mission. Such a bizarre collision of realities: cheap Chinese food and little wavy critters. He laughed and laughed, feeling like he was in a crazy dream.

Its eye opened and shut; a serious gesture that killed the comedy of it. Jason snapped to attention.

The idea was pretty obvious, simple.

With Big Mama now a deceased stain on the concrete outside, Jason had been anointed the parental duties of feeding the young budding . . .

*Sluglettes? Sluppies? Slittens? What are baby slugs called?*

He picked the orange chicken off the rack and the creature made a quick, happy motion of whizzing around his chest. It floated out in front of him leading him back to the laundry room.

He carried the disgusting container of rotting food and dumped it into the washing machine. He threw the empty container out of the window and immediately heard a flurry of activity inside the washer, as much as one would expect from thirty or forty thick slugs.

Big Mama dashed out into the den again. Jason followed. Still, three more cartons of Chinese food left.

There were many hungry babies to feed.

He had considered getting a pet many times. *You got your wish, buddy*. Fish, he liked fish: pretty colorful fish. Maybe a salamander, little painted turtles, or one of those teeny tiny frogs. Cute things that hop, swim or sleep on rocks. But never slugs. Slugs were weird and ugly.

The more he fed them, the more noise they made; frenzied wet disgusting slurps. Many slurps layered upon each other, amplified by the hollow metal casing of the washer.

*Yeech. Super Yeech.*

Luckily the raucous digital techno music blasting from his cell phone distracted him from possibly having to vomit.

He ran into the den, frisking his coat pockets to find it. He clicked it on.

"Jason. Where in the world are you? You were supposed to be here over an hour ago."

Roger, his least favorite person in the world. He sounded angry. When Roggie-boy was angry at someone, he sounded the most confident and focused, like it was something he relished more than anything.

"I traded shifts with Robert. I'm supposed to work for him on Saturday."

"Robert. No wonder! Didn't you know you have to get approval from a manager before you trade shifts with someone?"

"Uh, nope," he admitted. "Besides, I had some important stuff to work out with my new apartment. It was really important."

"Well, that's not my problem. We all got worries, brother. The store is likely to be busy later on so I'm going to have to insist that you hustle on down here. You know how short-handed we've been lately."

*We all got problems, Rog.* He wanted to say. *If the miserly store would hire enough people, full-time workers, not part-timers who don't care, we wouldn't be shorthanded all the time.*

Jason sighed into the phone.

"I'll cut you a deal. If you show up within the hour, I'll reward you by not writing you up. That would be your third write-up. One more write-up and it's adios amigo for you. I don't think you want that."

Jason took a deep breath.

"Sorry if I'm being a little harsh," Roger said, in his fake human tone.

"We've been slammed this morning. I got a monster of a headache. Please just show up."

"Okay."

He hung up. Calling Roger every foul name he could think of, he ran into his room to dress. He fished around the heaps of clothing on his bedroom floor for his name tag.

His second write-up. He had worked there almost two years. He had never called in sick. He was never late, more than five minutes anyway, and that was usually caused by traffic. Jason thought it was safe to gamble on Robert, figuring any past transgressions were smoothed over by now.

Roger was threatening another write-up?

That last write-up was under some dodgy circumstances. Jason had been five minutes late coming back from his fifteen minute break. Worse than that, during that five minutes, he had been in the doorway of the store talking with a customer he was friends with. So technically he could argue that he had been working at the time.

But no, Roger pointed out; he had been on cashier duty at the time so the excuse would have worked if he had been closer to the check-out section. Just fifteen feet closer.

Jason knew the real reason. He was currently the longest lasting full-time worker, raking in a whopping 75 cents more than the other suckers.

75 cents. After two years.

Lucky for the store, the managers could invent clever excuses to write-up employees that made too much money. They were allotted a certain budget from the corporate headquarters. Whatever money they saved came back to them in bonuses at the end of the year.

What a system!

Such blatant treachery, but that was how our modern society functioned, Jason guessed. It was even good in a way. It kept him from becoming an all-too-complacent retail worker. It reminded Jason that he needed to better himself or he'd wind up like Roger.

They weren't slammed that day, nor had they been that morning, as he gathered from his co-worker, a part-timer. He was a fairly new guy named Ricky or Richard. Ricky meandered the Political Science section, looking barely awake, a stack of crisp trade papers on a dolly beside him.

Jason quizzed him endlessly. He was becoming paranoid that Roger was screwing with him. Surely, managers were discouraged from playing mind games with their underlings. There had to be laws against that.

"If you could guess," he asked the new kid. "How many customers would you say we've had all morning?"

"I don't know. Twenty or thirty maybe. Dude, they don't pay me to stand around and inventory customers."

"But if the store had been *slammed,* you would know, right? The term *slammed* is pretty cut-and-dry."

"I've been too busy shelving to notice."

*Nice cop-out.*

The kid was one of them that shelved a lot because he lacked the work experience, or the motivation, to do anything else. He would have noticed if the store was busy because he would have started drooling or wetting himself. Jason slunk away shaking his head.

Roger had just been a lying jerk. Luckily, Captain Smug was done with his shift around two o'clock, so Jason didn't have to see him and stare pointed daggers at him all day.

He got another text from Carlos.

**DON'T B AVOIDING ME YOU KNW U OWE ME 4 BILLS**

Jason called him on his lunch break.

"Don't worry, Carlos. I get paid tomorrow. I'll stop by your place tomorrow, cash in hand. I want to see the bill statements though, all fair and square."

"OK. Remember, you didn't buy toilet paper or paper towels this month or last month. I might have to tack on a little extra."

"*Wrong*. I bought all those things last mouth. This month I had to save for my security deposit. Hey, Carlos, I was planning to literally *shower* the apartment with toilet paper and paper towels next month but you *had* to kick me out so suddenly."

"You can't keep using that excuse."

"Sure, I can. Just bring the bill statements. No funny stuff."

Jason gleefully rocked back in the break room chair. He loved this.

"I still haven't found the can opener, you know," Carlos said.

"Surely, you're not still whining about that."

"You bet I am! You stole it!"

"You can be so petty sometimes."

"I looked all around for it. It's not here."

"Did you check everywhere? Are you sure? Sometimes you open cans in the den. You should check in the couch."

"Don't get smart."

"Hey, Carlos. When's your birthday?"

"Two months ago."

"Oh no. That's too bad!"

Carlos grumbled.

"Hey, then, *next* year I'll buy you a new can opener! How's that sound?"

"I'm done with you, Jason. Have the money tomorrow."

"I'll meet you at your place. Have the statements ready."

"Shut up."

***

He spent a brief night at the Urban Turban, hanging out with a few other random people he knew. His co-worker, Melanie, showed up, a short giggly girl that slightly got on his nerves. He managed to sustain a conversation with her. Afterwards, he went to the diner.

The sounds of myriad creatures slurping on rotten Chinese food were still fresh; in fact, he had been hearing it in his mind all day. It made him think of huge squishy maggots. And the smell . . . a sour afterbirth smell, mixed with the chemical odor of laundry detergent seemed to cling to the inside of his nostrils.

He went home late.

# CHAPTER 3

HE HAD TO be at work the same time the next day: eleven o'clock. Retail hours were murder. Four thirty some days, eleven o'clock other days. Nine am some days.

After he got dressed and grabbed his bag, he saw Big Mama. Right after he opened the door. She startled him.

In the doorway was a greenish blue circle with its golden piercing eye. Jason gave a hand circle back, half-heartedly this time. As he descended the front step the circle became a **q**.

A normal **q**. It was pointing at the ground.

A dead squirrel was there, half rotted. Its smell was strong.

*Sorry, honey. No time. Got to go to work.*

As he was unlocking his car door, Big Mama tried to beckon him down the road. There must have been a carcass around, a dead deer in the woods, maybe a mulch heap too, anything disgusting and rotted. They did eat vegetables, as evidenced by the lack of green peppers and carrot chips in his washer.

They weren't picky.

Anything was yummy as long as it was sour and rotten.

In the car during the drive to work, Big Mama hovered over the dashboard. When they apparently got close to some dead animal, or something rotten, Big Mama would expand and shrink; a big **O** then a small **o**, a big **O** then a small **o . . .** meaning he needed to stop.

Feed my babies. Work can wait. My babies need food.

He almost drove off the road a few times. Horns blared as he swiped at the circular thing.

*Not now. Please God, not now.*

Big O. Small o . . .

*Please, God, get lost.*

***

He didn't see Big Mama the rest of the day. She had merely whisked herself away about a mile from his job.

During his thirty minute food break, he cashed his check at a nearby bank and texted Carlos again. He wanted to confirm that he was coming over there right after work. They still needed to set an approximate time.

He eagerly waited for this day. The glorious sound of trumpets would blast; a thousand string orchestra would hum, angels would soar to the heavens. This was the day he would finally sever ties with his old bastard of an ex-roommate.

It was like some kind of rite of passage to his new life, a coronation to some new wonderful stage.

By the time he got out of work, Carlos had sent him a text:

CHANGE OF PLAN I WANT 2 MEET U AT UR PLACE

I KNW WHERE UR PLACE IS

THAT PLACE IS A DUMP HA HA

I GOT THE BILLS ALL WORKED OUT NICE N NEAT

*Oh. My. God.*

He had been worried about familiar people visiting his house so soon with the squirmies hanging around. More than that, he was worried that Carlos was going to see the squalid apartment complex he lived in and mock him. Maybe he wouldn't, if he wasn't feeling cocky. If Jason was lucky Carlos would give him something vaguely condescending.

*Bullshit. You've got him fired up lately. He's going to revel in this.*

Jason wouldn't be surprised if Carlos took pictures of it. He could easily see Carlos taking pictures of his place and putting it all over his Facebook page with captions like: *Look at the shithole my can opener stealing ex-roommate lives in! Look at this rusty refrigerator in the front yard!*

Carlos would do that.

Then the stupid feud would go on and on to infinity.

***

When Jason arrived home, he frantically began clearing as much trash out of the front yard as fast as he could, shucking everything into the huge plastic garbage cans. He was fully aware of how lousy it all looked, what a trashy low-life dump he lived in.

Unfortunately, he couldn't budge the junky refrigerator, a corner of it buried deep, nearly fossilized, melded with the ground.

Carlos didn't pull up until around 9:30 that night. Jason was ready to get this over with. The wad of cash burned in his hand as he leaned over the wooden railings, waiting. He thumped down the steps as soon as Carlos pulled up.

Carlos stepped around the front of the car. Jason flung out the wad of bills.

"Here ya go. Fifty bucks. That ought to cover everything."

"Whoa. That's way too much."

"Take it. I don't care. I just want us to be squared up."

"Really?"

"That speech you gave about me not buying toilet paper really tugged my heartstrings."

"Aw. That's sweet."

A big toothy grin emerged from Carlos's mouth. It was eerie to see him with a sense of humor.

"I bet you're really generous to the crack heads that come around. You probably give them free rocks, don't you?"

"Of course," Jason said. "I have my own local outreach center in my den."

"You are truly an inspirational figure in this community. You know what would just top this evening off? If I could take a look inside your luxurious apartment!"

"Okay. The joke's over. Take the money and split, Carlos. I've had a long day."

"Undoubtedly, you are exhausted from all your charity work and civic functions."

Carlos grinned and nudged him with his elbow.

"Show me around."

"Take the money and beat it, Carlos. I'm serious."

"What? You didn't prepare any red wine or hors d'oeuvres? Shame on you."

Carlos began charging up the yard, towards the door.

Jason chased him up the stairs. He cursed himself for not shutting the door all the way. If he had, Carlos's subterfuge would have been foiled. The jerk swooped right in. He pointed at the duct-taped lawn chairs, cackling like a crazy man.

"You're so damn *poor*! It's a pity you have to live like this. I don't mean to laugh, but, you know, I *have to*."

"Great, Carlos. Congratulations."

"Seriously, though. I'm just going use your bathroom and then split. That's okay, right?"

"Yeah, sure. Hurry up."

"You have one, right?"

Jason forced a mock laugh, "Yeah. Just go straight and turn left."

"All right."

He walked a few paces then whipped around, pointing, grinning.

"Fooled you! Ha ha!" he shouted. "I came here to take back what you stole!"

He darted into the kitchen, squealing laughter. Jason could hear drawers flying open, cabinets bumping open and shut.

"Then take it," said Jason. "You're the one with no class. You evicted me virtually on the spot. Think I like living in this dump? I don't!"

Objects shifted in the drawers, as Carlos mumbled. His sneakers squeaked on the tiles.

"Ah *ha*! Busted! These forks look familiar too."

Carlos waved the can opener in his face. He did a stupid little victory dance, grinning.

"I knew it! I knew it! You *stole* it."

"Good for you. Take it and scram."

"I will! You're damned right, you dirty thief—"

Carlos's wide mocking mouth suddenly disappeared under a flash of dark green. Jason jumped back.

Choking sounds and muffled screams came from the man.

It was wasn't dark green. It was greenish blue.

The creatures were attacking him.

Two more flew onto his face, sticking there like huge globs of greenish-blue jelly. Jelly that had a mind of its own. They clamped down tight, flattening themselves against his face.

Jason jumped back again as Carlos flailed violently, flinging his arms out, a rope of bloody drool whipping this way and that. Horrible gurgling sounds, puffing cheeks, red eyes. Within a minute, Carlos crashed to the floor, his beloved white baseball jacket becoming a Jackson Pollack painting splattered with red and purple.

Another half a minute of thrashing and spasms then he was still.

Jason went cold.

It was the first time he had ever seen a corpse.

Light-headedness. Then sleep. How long? Jason wasn't sure.

He was lying on the floor of the den and there was vomit on his shirt. Vomit in his mouth.

Around the wall from where he sat, a pair of sneakers pointed up.

There was a dead body in his kitchen. This was one predicament he never expected to be in. As a kid, he couldn't even keep a fish aquarium because he got too upset when the fish floated to the top. He couldn't stand to see dead bugs.

When his grandmother passed away two years ago. he couldn't look at the open coffin in the funeral house. Handling death wasn't a skill of his.

Maybe not dead?

He crept into the kitchen and took another peek. Carlos's face had turned a grayish color.

Definitely, certifiably dead. Dead as in no heartbeat, no brain activity, no breathing. Carlos had no spark of life. He was a corpse.

He is deceased, passed away, departed, reposed, bereft of life, cadaverous, inanimate, perished, resting in peace, and dead as a doornail. Carlos checked out, bought the farm, kicked the bucket, and had gone to meet his maker. He was put out of his misery. He shuffled off the mortal coil. He was sleeping the Big Sleep.

He was dead and, worst of all, *on Jason's floor.*

The slug things crawled across Carlos's chest and face. Not eating him, thank God.

Not yet. He wasn't ripe enough.

More slugs were arriving. Six or seven were cruising up his body, meandering, perhaps waiting until the body was at the right stage.

Jason's mind raced. He knew he had to do something fast.

*I'm not a murderer. I didn't kill this guy. In fact I tried to stop him from coming into the apartment.*

It was Carlos's fault. He walked right into it. Pride did this to him.

*You died over a can opener. They're going to have a field day with you in the afterlife.*

It wasn't about evading a murder rap, hiding the body, or coming up with an excuse for the cops. It was more about not having to endure the sounds of tiny gooey monsters slurping on a corpse.

More of them were on the wall, trekking in a line towards the corpse.

Not much time.

He fished out some large green trash bags from under the sink. The first one went over the head and torso of the stiffening body. The second went over the legs. Still, this left about a foot and a half of middle section showing. More trash bags and tape. Jason worked on this more meticulously than anything he had ever done, and had exerted more focus on this task than he was normally capable.

Fifteen minutes later, he had constructed a tightly sealed body bag for his ex-roommate.

*A body bag.*

What a hideous expression. It wasn't even a bag. A proper body bag was at least neat and somber.

He dragged the body into the bathroom, his stomach pitching at the feel of loose flesh and bone under his grip. He never thought Carlos was this heavy. He never thought *anybody* was this heavy.

Jason sent his mind somewhere far away. *I'm just loading a dead deer into the back of my dad's truck. Like that time when I was fifteen and dad hit one on the way to the hardware store. Daddy made me load it up, laughing at the funny faces of revulsion I was making. Maybe it's firewood, not dead flesh. A huge log, a gooey, sweaty, human smelling log that dad wanted to chop up to try out his new axe.*

At last he wrestled him into the bathtub.

Slug things were swarming in. He saw several were already cruising around the plastic coffin seeking an entry spot.

Jason used his fingers to break two holes in the plastic. The slug creatures slithered into it in an orderly fashion, thankfully not enough to break the plastic more.

Then Jason bolted out of there.

Big Mama hovered in the den, in a big circle with the golden eye lingering on top.

"OK, my ass," he said to it. "I have a corpse in my bathroom now. Please get out of here."

Big Mama unraveled into a wispy line.

"Do you understand what *Go* means?"

He drew the word Go in the air with his finger and pointed out the door. "Go. Get out. I want you and your whole disgusting family out of my house."

Jason fished his keys out of his pocket and dashed outside.

It was time to flee the madhouse.

He didn't go to the diner. He just drove around. He was too frantic; his mind spinning in circles. Like a pinwheel in a hurricane.

*I should have called the cops.*

He definitely looked like a murderer now. If he had just left the corpse alone, the cops would have seen the critters in his mouth and he would have been exonerated from blame.

*This was Mike Shibble's or Sandra Millman's fault.*

She probably was some kind of underground exotic pet smuggler. Maybe she worked for the government. Maybe the creatures were some kind of Area 51 experiment gone awry. Sandra Millman was hiding out. Some men in dark suits, with pistols in their coats, would show up, cap his ass, and haul away the experimental animals.

*I don't deserve to go to jail.* He kept seeing himself in an interrogation room, beefy street-wise cops hammering him with questions, trying to break him down and make him confess.

He saw himself in an orange jumpsuit, his face all over the news.

He tried to contemplate this from a law and order viewpoint as he hit Highway I-20 going towards Atlanta. Just driving. He would cruise up to another exit, then maybe turn back.

What was done was done. The blame would fall wherever. He was out of his depths here.

His real problem was in his bathtub. His real problem was a one hundred and sixty pound hunk of organic matter soon to be rotting and stinking.

A former human being that used to talk, walk, sing in the shower, comb his hair, paint, complain, speak Spanish, and wear a girly beige bathrobe around the house...

*This is all I need right now.*

*Sorry, Carlos.*

*You idiot.*

It was going to take those monsters several days to devour the body. There was a lot of him they would be able to eat.

Lots of leftovers.

*I prefer not to think about that.*

He would have to dispose of it. But how? There was a lake near his house; the McCullen's place. No, scratch that. It was too close by. There was a better one near his mom's house, miles away in Griffin. It was very secluded. He could wrap it up in a tarp and dump it.

*That seems really easy in the movies, Jason. But you'll fuck it up.*

He could barely look at it without gagging. Hell, he could barely lift the sucker.

*I'm a novel and comics nerd, not a digging-a-shallow-grave-by-moonlight kind of guy.*

There was the issue of his car, too. How would he get rid of that? What would an Alfred Hitchcock character do?

Ixnay on that. Alfred Hitchcock characters usually got caught.

On the plus side, Carlos didn't have much of a social life. Most likely no one knew he had been going over to Jason's in the first place. He had one estranged girlfriend who was in college but Jason wasn't sure of their current status. Most likely, they split up completely. He was quite certain they hadn't spoken in a while.

Carlos's parents were retired in Honduras. He had no family stateside that Jason knew of.

As he drove, he dug around for his cell phone.

End this madness. Call the cops.

*This situation has way too many variables for you to handle. Give it up, homey.*

His phone wasn't in his pockets, or anywhere in the car. It was at his house.

Jason drove back.

# CHAPTER 4

CARLOS STOOD IN the middle of his den.

It was almost Carlos anyway, the dead Carlos.

He couldn't technically be called a zombie. A standing dead person was what he looked like.

There might not be a name for it.

He swayed on his feet. About ten of the slug creatures lined his shoulders and arms. His mouth was stuffed with them. One clung to his ear.

Behind him, looped around his foot and trailing on the floor, was the shredded plastic body bag.

Big Mama, shaped as a sideways **P**, hovered waist level. Jason understood. He dug into Carlos's pocket and pulled out his car keys, the plastic keychain advertising the language school he worked at. The grayish dead hand was already open and waiting, suspended there. The fingers weakly closed around them. The keys started to tumble out. Jason tucked them back in.

*They could control his brain; weakly, but they could. How bizarre, hideously and disgustingly bizarre.*

In nature, certain types of parasites can do this, certain types of wasps to be specific. Jason remembered reading about a breed of parasites infecting mice. They take over the mouse's brain and make them attracted to cats. Then a cat eats them. Then the parasite has a bigger host.

Crafty little buggers.

Maybe the slug thing sticking to Carlos's ear was playing a big role in this.

Carlos lumbered out the door like a drunken Frankenstein but with surprising skill. Jason followed him down the steps. The critters inside him navigated quite well. Big Mama was probably the biggest contributor, encircling his head like a greenish blue halo, beaming like a thick band instead of just a wispy line as if in deep concentration.

It brightened and dimmed with struggle. Her little gold eye was beaming like a light, like a miniature coal miner's helmet.

Carlos's face was grayish and sagging a bit. His thinning black hair stood up in tiny tufts devoid of the LA Lakers cap.

The Franken-Carlos lumbered towards his parked car. Jason darted his head around. Even though Carlos could be mistaken for a drunk, the morons in room 5 might see this and create a spectacle out of it. Jason could imagine them leaning over the banister, heckling and pointing, flecks of bong residue fresh on their shitty little mouths.

Thankfully the outside was dead silent.

*Got to be careful. I'm not out of the woods yet.*

Carlos even opened the door by himself. Almost. Weak fingers fumbled at the handle.

Jason told him to back up.

"Let me get it."

The cab light came on. Jason guided him in and helped find the right key. Jason stuck it in the ignition and started the car up. Hands flopped over the steering wheel.

Jason squeezed the fingers onto the steering wheel to make sure they were tight. Chills. *Carlos's hands are so cold.* Jason was reminded again that he was dealing with a corpse. The bizarre nature of the predicament kept shielding this fact from him.

In the dim cab light, Jason accidentally glanced at it. His heart raced.

*Keep your head in the game, J.*

The engine whooshed.

Too much gas.

"Take it easy."

He pointed to his own foot, staring at Big Mama. A little demonstration. He raised his foot, then eased it down slowly.

"Gently, please. Like this. Not so hard."

The car lurched forward then stopped. Brake lights flashed on. It lurched forward again. Jason saw the windshield wipers come on. The car inched out into the road. Ten feet later, it gained speed. It zigzagged as it got further down the road.

Surprisingly, it kept going until the taillights disappeared.

***

They were gone, just like that.

Not completely. Ten or fifteen of them still meandered around the rim of the washing machine, some inside of it. Jason groaned. As usual, a few of them raised up when they saw him, one launched onto his elbow, spry and nimble as a cricket. He peeled it off and tossed it into the washer.

*What in God's name are you things?*

Two more jumped onto his arm, not aggressively but, well, *lovingly*, the tips of their little heads, craning up to him.

Such cute little murderers.

*You are evil creatures. You are not natural.* Invertebrate creatures don't hop onto humans like little playful kittens. He couldn't even tell if they had vertebras or not.

Could science even classify them?

You're not supposed to have those tiny yellow speck eyes. Why did they have two eyes? Their mommy only had one. It didn't make sense. Nature was supposed to, at least, be normal on the surface.

He saw two of the sluglettes connected together, rolling around, rocking back and forth, tails slapping, playing like little frisky puppies.

That's not natural behavior.

*You are some kind of secret experiment created in a lab.*

He read a lot of science magazines, often took home old copies from work after their covers were stripped. He knew scientists were doing all kinds of DNA splicing with animals these days. They could create new breeds of animals, called Chimeras, with some wacky genetic tinkering. A while back he had seen a freaky picture of a donkey and zebra hybrid . . . called a Zonkey!

And there was cloning. Today's scientific community was on fire with the concept of cloning: cloning sheep, cloning rats, dogs, alligators . . .

If they are doing things like that and publishing their results in mainstream magazines, God knows what else they were doing in secret.

Hence, these little monstrosities.

Intelligent slugs? Shape shifting gastropods? Area 51 stuff, aliens, other dimensions, all possible, all out there, in their discreet underground laboratories. Everybody is aware these things go on, but reality keeps us grounded to the more routine, knowable aspects of life. It's what keeps us sane.

Even science couldn't be blamed. Having DNA at all meant they were mostly natural.

Jason zeroed in on one of the sluglettes by itself on one corner of the washer. It was vibrating, slowly at first, then quicker, so that its whole body distorted into a blue green squiggle. Jason could barely focus his eyes on it. It thinned out as it vibrated turning into a shimmering green line.

Only for a second. Its normal form suddenly reappeared, flattening out against the blue painted metal of the washer. It was still. It was resting.

Looking up, he saw another sluglette doing this on the very tip top of the washing machine lid where it was open and cocked back. This critter was doing the same thing: shimmering, vibrating, turning into a little line and then going still.

He knew what was happening. They were like little baby birds trying to take that first leap into adulthood: flight. Soon all of them would be able to shape shift into shiny little lines and whizz around the air like their mama.

These things were so unnatural. Scratch that! Unnatural was a term too good for them. Satanic. Satanic was better.

Jason picked each one off of the machine and tossed them into the washer tub. He checked around it and picked up a few more. He picked one off the wall. One was on his shoulder about to crawl around his back.

He tossed them all into the tub.

He shut the lid. Or he tried to. Three of them flew up to the top and jutted out. He poked them back in with his finger. He slammed the lid down.

He picked up the box of detergent from the floor.

*This should kill them.*

He decided he should dump the whole box into it and bury them under it. Then he could spray some Raid into the mix. Poison them.

Good idea. A quick humane death.

Just keeping the lid down would probably suffocate them.

*Kill these hideous satanic creatures.*

As soon as they developed the ability to transform into those squiggly lines, maybe they would be impossible to kill.

*It's now or never.*

They were making thumping noises against the lid of the washer, some barely audible squeaking sounds of panic came from within like distant duck callers, *wak wak wak . . .*

He couldn't kill them. He was a wimp. He couldn't kill animals and he certainly couldn't kill baby animals. He couldn't bear to see their wet jelly bodies convulsing in death throes, gushing pus-like fluids, their little speck eyes popping out oozing God-knows-what all into the gears and circuits of his washing machine.

That would surely leave a smell, a rotting smell. Too many rotting smells in his life these days.

Rotting like Carlos would soon be doing in his little Toyota Celica.

*Don't think about that.*

The smell, the smell of his dead sluggies, would linger and remind him of this horrible night.

. . . and he'd have to clean it out, scoop and scrape and scrub the slug carcasses out, heaving and gagging.

*I could sure use my dad right now.*

His dad had been a go-to kind of guy, an action man, with his squinty eyes and a dark black beard always so neat and perfectly manicured that it seemed stenciled on his jaws and lips. His dad ate sardines with Tabasco sauce for breakfast and spoke in choppy sentences. If there was a wasp nest forming where it wasn't supposed to be, dad would bat that sucker to Hell post-haste.

He didn't even care if a wasp came after him when the deed was done. He wouldn't flinch but squash the vermin with his bare, already callused, hands. Jason had seen it.

*He'd know what to do.* When Jason was ten years old, he had seen his dad in the kitchen smash a huge rat with a crowbar with ninja speed. Didn't think twice, just started clobbering away. Jason had to clean it up with a shovel and paper towels while his dad strutted back to the den to watch the Georgia Bulldogs whip some ass.

"*Just kill those things, ya dang sissy!* Daddy's voice played in his mind. *Sissy*, that was a dad word. And pretty apt. Dad wouldn't let these things have the run of the house, not for a day, nor an hour, nor a second. Big Daddy Wylie would take charge, nuke those bastards into slug butter then go into the kitchen and make a jam and mayonnaise sandwich.

Poor little Jason Wylie couldn't.

There were other reasons, good reasons. These weren't wasps or rats or any ordinary creatures. The ones that were stuck to Carlos would probably come back anyway and render his efforts futile. Big Mama would definitely exact some revenge if she found her litter decimated at her return.

Satanic or not, they would remain alive. In some weird

way, they probably were natural. They need to eat, right? If they ate, they pooped. Pooping equals natural.

They probably breathe air. They were limited in some ways to natural laws, so maybe they were natural.

If they existed and the Lord saw it fit for them to be squirming around in his laundry room, then they deserved to live.

He flipped up the lid.

He slunk into the kitchen and opened the refrigerator. *Might as well feed the little parasites.* There were some rotting stir fry in the back, a container that predated the Orange Chicken by about two days. This was the last container.

Walking back to the laundry room he thought a second then stopped. He went back into the kitchen and picked out all the bits of shrimp.

*No meat for you.* Sorry, kiddies, only vegetables. If they ate humans, which he hoped they didn't, maybe he had a chance to reverse it. Maybe. That would be a Godsend. It would probably improve their smell also.

He always noticed the faint rotting odor when he first came into the apartment. It became especially apparent to him after spending a while in the laundry room. The little critters were smelling bad, a stinky rotten kind of bad.

After dumping the container into the washing machine, he felt a sleepy sensation wash over him. The image of Carlos standing there returned. He felt a swoon, his knees buckling.

He eased down on his den floor and went to sleep, or maybe passed out, with the lights on.

***

He awoke later, startled awake. Big Mama was in the center of the room, staring at him, in her huge thick form, a graceful whale shape, like how whales were depicted in cartoons anyway. He saw that her tail was shaking. He expected anything from her.

An urge struck him to run out. Or grab something.

*She is going to kill you.*

The stare.

*That shuddering tail thing is new. I wonder what it means.*

He clamped his eyes shut as she slithered up to him, climbed onto his lap and onto his chest. He waited for a quick death, but all he felt was an exasperated shutter from her slick warm body. She wanted him to wake up, but was perturbed when he kept laying there, insensate and limp.

He was playing possum. And he intended to keep playing possum.

Something had gone wrong with the meat chauffer. She pressed against him and wiggled her strange skin against his cheek, urging him to awaken.

*Sorry, babe, but this is your problem. They're your kids and they brought this on themselves. They can't go to prison, I can.*

He kept at this until her heaviness vanished all at once. Opening one eye, he saw her transform back into a squiggly line and shoot out of the room.

That was the last he saw of her that night.

# CHAPTER 5

**HE DID CLEANING** the next day.

There was nothing like having a dead body in your house to inspire some real cleaning. He mainly used Windex. It was all he had at the moment. If he left the house to get real cleaning products, he might be confronted with Carlos's corpse. He didn't want a shred of suspicion from the law.

Windex would get the job done: Windex on everything. Ammonia and water equals clean. As soon as he had the time, he would shampoo the carpets. He'd look into it later on. Right now, the carpet got shampooed with Windex.

The slug babies often left light green secretions that easily evaporated, but in thick concentrations it hardened into white dust. Probably only he could see this. The non-trained eye would miss it. Jason knew his babies well.

In the back of his mind, he wondered how far the corpse drove. As the morning drifted towards noon, Big Mama still hadn't reappeared.

Maybe the thing caused an accident, and plowed into a bus. It could have caused a multi-car pileup, ripped through a playground or smashed into a hospital and exploded. There were so many awful things a bad driver could do.

*Don't concern yourself.*

He wanted to just act normal. That last thing he needed to do was act suspicious. He had to look out for number one. Carlos stepped into this himself. All Jason wanted, from the very beginning, was to be rid of him. Whatever happened was Carlos's fault, that shithead.

*Don't be a pendejo over Carlos.*

Carlos threw that word around quite often. It was his favorite word, savoring it in his mouth like his mom's home cooking when he got a chance to use it on him. 'Why do you have to ruffle the rug when you come in, pendejo?' 'Damn, pendejo, wash that glass out when you're finished!'

*Who's the pendejo now, **pendejo**?*

Maybe police would question him. After all, Carlos was on his way to Jason's house. It was possible no one was aware of it. It was such mundane shit there was no reason to post a bulletin about it.

Yet somewhere down the line, he suspected a cop would question him about the incident.

Hopefully with no suspicion of foul play.

That afternoon, his phone rang. It was Janet from work.

"Hey, Jason. Robert didn't show up. Weren't you supposed to work for him?"

"Kind of. We agreed on it. When he didn't show up for me, I thought the plan was null and void."

"Oh, well. He's not here and I was hoping you'd come in. We need an extra person."

*Please, tell me this is a joke.*

He wasn't going to get off so easy after all.

Jason agreed to come in. He did want to get out of the house. Besides, he reckoned, if Carlos's corpse turned up in some strange place, he would appear less suspicious stocking shelves and answering phones at work.

He drove a different route to work. He had to keep his mind clear.

*Don't think about the cruising corpse.*

Unfortunately for him, Roger was the night manager.

Jason went right along scanning his section in a surprisingly good mood, happy to be away from squiggly monsters and dead people.

Poor Roger had his work cut out for him tonight. He was no happy camper. He had to deal with several two-bit scammers trying to return goods they obviously never purchased from the store, demanding cash refunds. That was the oldest trick in the book. Poor little Roger flittered hither and yon, on the phone, squinting over receipts and checks, all red-faced.

The store was crime central. An action packed Saturday night at The Book Barn. The store detective busted a thief in the back with three books in his pants and one in his coat. A drunk passed out in the bathroom and unloaded in the stall. Roger had to mop it up. The Casanova security guard lingered in front of the store hitting on high school girls. In the art book section, Jason witnessed two guys sneakily engaged in a marijuana sale.

Co-workers grumbled and sighed, and mumbled complaints about customers under their breaths while customers jabbered loudly on cell phones, leaving behind piles of magazines and books, empty coffee cups and half-eaten cookies, cakes, and muffins.

Jason felt fine. He felt great, in a superficial way. He had lively conversations with co-workers and customers. Under the surface, a slight otherworldly feeling simmered, like he had awoke from a weird dream.

*Maybe I'll drag some folks out to the Urban Turban. That's the ticket. Have some fun.*

He thought about the vibrating sluglettes on his washer, trying to take flight. It was something hopeful. Maybe they would all start vibrating stronger soon and fly away, fly far away. The sooner the better.

He longed for the time when he would have a normal apartment and could invite friends over. The place needed to be anointed with some good ole human mirth for a change.

He planned to call Dave after work at least. Get the details about his slick little score from two nights ago.

A part-timer Melanie asked him out. Not really a "date"

kind of out. Or maybe it was. She was flirty with him but not quite readable. Her roommate was having a birthday party. The problem was her roommate was new in town and didn't have too many friends. She said she was inviting anyone she could.

"Please, come. Bring some friends. I'm trying to break her out of her shell."

*Brings friends? I have friends? You mean both of them?*

He said he'd try.

***

He was working a mid-shift. He clocked out at seven with itchy feet. He was still riding high on his feeling of liberation.

Before he could exit the door, he had to stop. He beeped. Its little red eye glared at him accusingly near the gift card rack. Roger, at the check-out desk, shot over to him.

Within seconds, Jason whisked the magnetic security tags out of his front shirt pocket. He had to put these in the merchandise in the back and often left some in his pocket. It happened with everybody once in a while.

"Got the culprits right here, Roggie, the usual suspects."

"Give me your coat. I'd rather not have to come over there and frisk you." Roger said smiling. "It's store policy, you know."

Jason glowered for a second then rolled his eyes.

"You can't be serious."

"Sorry, buddy. Rules are rules."

He handed it over. Roger dug through it thoroughly, humming. *Asshole.* Roger tossed it back with a satisfied glint in his eye.

"You're clean, kiddo," Roger gave him one of his cheese ball salutes, "Have a good one!"

Jason headed out, quite miffed.

The whole exchange happened quickly. Jason didn't notice that when Roger saluted him, he had a greenish blue lump on his sleeve.

Jason got a phone call thirty minutes later.

"Roger's dead!" said Melanie. "He choked to death on some sushi he picked up. He died right in the break room. Ambulances were here, cops . . . total chaos. You sure left at the right time."

"You're kidding! He's definitely dead?"

"The EMTs confirmed it as soon as they checked him out."

"That's insane."

"Oh, my God! It was—"

Suddenly, a horn blatted behind him. He wasn't sure if it was meant for him or not. He stopped at a red light, still talking with Melanie. He looked to his right and saw the driver beside him in a sporty red convertible. The guy who had been blowing the horn, glared back at him. He was muttering something.

"Hold on a sec, Mel."

He muffled the phone to his chest.

"What?"

"Hang up that thing and drive, why don't you!" The guy spat, wind blowing through his hair. "You were going twenty miles an hour back there!"

"I don't normally do this! I hate cell phones. Give me a break, man! My friend just died."

"Yeah, right. You idiot!"

The light turned green. The angry man shot forward. Jason shouted expletives. Oh, don't people just love to insult you and cruise away? Shithead. So, you're a perfect driver all the time? Never made a mistake?

On the angry driver's back door, Jason saw greenish blue blots. Slug things! On his own door, on the passenger side, crawled three more.

*They were in his coat*. It was wadded up in the passenger seat, flopped open. The inside lining had a tear in it. Several sluglettes could easily stow away without him noticing. He had to hustle out the door earlier this afternoon and didn't think to check.

He finally figured it out.

It was about revenge.

*These things go after anyone who makes me angry. This isn't all about eating. I control them.*

Carlos, Roger, even a random road rage jerk. The clearest example had been last night, after Carlos died. He had told them to get out and they commandeered a corpse to do exactly that.

Steadfast loyalty.

As he got closer to his neighborhood, he heard police sirens and a static-laden voice over a police radio. As he drove closer, he saw four or five squad cars parked on the road, lights swirling. There had been a car accident, perhaps something crazier.

Jason spotted the tail-end of Carlos's tan Yaris parked in a house.

*In a house*

Bricks, shingles and glass buried the front of it. From where Jason was, it looked like it had smashed into the porch. Two tracks of black dirt and uprooted grass trailed over a demolished chain-link fence then downhill slightly, ending at the house. The corpse was a worse driver than Jason thought.

Someone had collapsed in the middle of the yard, face down. It was obvious who this was.

Gun shots erupted from the house. A scream. Curtains fluttered at a window. A group of cops were huddled near the fence. They looked confused and anxious, the sergeant waving his arms and shouting at them.

A big beefy black policeman ran up to Jason's car, a radio in his hand.

"Get the hell out of here," he told Jason.

"What's going on?"

"Oh, nothing much. See that house with the dead person in the front yard? We're going in there in a few minutes to watch the Super bowl!" The cop sneered at Jason. "Something went crazy in there. Just get lost!"

The cop spotted the slug creature on the inside of the door. His eyes widened.

"It's one of those *things*!"

A second later two slugs jumped up and latched themselves onto the cop's face. He shot backwards, thrashing wildly, screaming.

Jason felt his head being pulled. Blindness. He couldn't see. He assumed it was another cop until he saw a greenish blue swirl whizzing before his eyes.

It was Big Mama. She was trying to pull him out of the car.

He basically didn't have a choice; her strength might decapitate him if he resisted. He shut off the car engine and flipped the handle of the door. Slowly, he could feel himself being under the control of Big Mama, taking over his body like she had done with Carlos.

Out of the car, it was like he imagined being in a tornado would feel, a mini-tornado: loss of control and spinning. This was mainly in his mind. Big Mama let up a bit and allowed him control of his feet. He could feel ground underneath them, dried leaves crunching, tiny sticks, roots, and mounds of dirt.

At last he could see. She was leading him by the head, a little more gently this time. Woods. She was taking him through the woods. There were a few acres of it near his apartment. Slowly, he got acclimatized to the sensation, had at least some idea of what was going on.

"Slow down, damn it!" he said to her, at least tried to, but it didn't get passed his cheeks.

*Don't break my neck. I'm going!*

Big Mama led him down the hilly ditch, his feet fumbled, his toes thudding over rocks, into big rocks, flipping some of them over. Dry straw and leaves collected at the arches of his feet. Then the soles of his shoes connected with flat ground, hobbling upon his tortured legs.

She was surrounding his head. The woods grew darker.

She spun faster around him. He felt his feet leave the ground. Trees rushed past, branches, leaves, even a briar or two whipped and slapped his body, scratching at his skin. He could easily hit a tree. Pinks, greens, blues and purples blinded him. A mulch wet smell filled his nostrils, sour woodsy sappy smell converging to further confuse his senses.

As they got deeper into the woods, the pulling and colors subsided. She was relaxing a bit, maybe assuming they were safe from the police or whatever might be pursuing them. He felt hard crunchy soil under his feet again, heard the shudder of tree limbs overhead, and rattling leaves. Birds were panicking and possibly squirrels too.

He felt top heavy and dizzy. The back of his neck throbbed.

He could see.

Big Mama floated out in front of him like a greenish blue serpent. She had let him go, let him rest. He didn't expect to be left alone for long. It was a wonder he could breathe with her swirling around his face like that, but he could, without the slightest feeling of suffocation. She was more like a silky strand than anything thick and obstructive.

She didn't give him much time to rest. She quickly covered his head again as he tried to scream in protest, but was merely dragged along.

Then things really got strange.

He was falling. Even though his body had been out of his own control for quite some time, he still had a ground underneath him. He could feel his body come in contact with familiar woodsy things. He wasn't prepared for the next stage. The ground just went away. Confused and blind he felt his whole material world, the only world he knew from birth until the present time, just vanish.

Gone. Bye-bye earth.

Coolness was all around him, the air feeling thinner, even cleaner with no smells. A world with no smells; no smells nor sounds. He could feel the hollowness of this new world immediately, a spacious cold abyss with no bottom, no top, no sides, no width, nothing measurable, at least nothing he could discern in his state. His physical body had been transformed into some kind of near weightless object: a leaf, a snowflake, a piece of string or even a chewing gum wrapper blown down an endless manhole.

He'd always had this fear as a child, afraid some worker would leave the cover off a manhole and he'd step into it. Well, now it finally happened.

Luckily, the falling didn't last long: his feet hit a surface, a familiar cold surface: rock. It was down-sloping, slick rock at that, the soles of his shoes were dragged across them. He wanted to reach out with his fingers but, even if he could, he was afraid his skin would be sheared off by the friction.

His ears grasped for sounds.

Nothingness, a void.

Down down down. Big Mama eased off of him, slowly until he was walking with his own legs. She was looped around his arm. He thought she had split in half, since he saw another version of her by his right arm.

Others joined in.

The ground flattened, down-sloped again, and again flattened. He felt tiny ridges in the rock, then bigger ridges, then the ridges became full-blown steps, not perfectly even or flat but they carried him upwards as steps do. His feet sloppily pounded on them as his vision began to improve.

*Light, oh my God, light.* His eyes hungered for light.

The space around him began to illuminate in electro-neon squiggly eels, multicolored lights stretched over infinity like a spaceship in a Sci-Fi film shooting into warp speed. Between this long laser light show, huge bodies of rock lay out before him in ancient silence: roundish, smooth and huge.

The colors were so bright they almost burned his eyes; colors dominated not only by greenish blue, but also reds and oranges and pinks, and violets and other assorted hues that merged and created others. A mish-mashed rainbow; a huge crystal blasted by powerful light.

The ground flatted. The laser rainbow wave gushed away in one large swathe. He felt his knees buckle and fell.

The rock underneath him felt cold and a little wet. His head spun with dizziness and he just sat there propped up on his hands.

It was as cold as a cast-iron cellar. It was now time for that all-important question: *Where the hell am I?*

Colorful light from above still illuminated things some. He flipped over into a sitting position, resting because his body insisted, not because he wanted to sit still. He would turn away and bolt if he could.

Through the racing light overhead, he made out his surroundings: caverns, caves, and smooth rock, revealing a slickness that dimly reflected the colors of the swimming things. He knew these types of caverns weren't typical in the region where he lived. North of the state had large underground caverns, famous ones that were made into amusement parks. There were some in the southern part. Southeast Georgia didn't have any.

*Welcome to extra-dimensional travel, Jason.* No unicorns, pixies, Hydras, or little green men. And no Cthulu nor Freddy Kruger. For another dimension, it was probably prosaic.

*At least I don't have to worry about bats.*

There were no cool stalagmites that he could see, no other kinds of familiar rock formations whose names were known only to tweed-coated college professors who gave monotone lectures on Geology. Looking up, he caught the sight of some possible stalactites but they were too far up for him to be certain.

What he could see was a literal sea of squigglies, like Big Mama's familiar form, gushing across, a beautiful sight actually. He couldn't tear his eyes off of the stunning scene. Blue serpents swam across the ceiling; some like snakes, some swam in circles, some crossed each other, and some swam slower.

Big Mama looped herself around his arm and coaxed him to his feet. After walking a bit more, she led him to the curving down-slope of the rock. He hesitated, afraid he would plunge into some kind of new abyss, into some other Alice-in-Wonderland level.

His heart would explode if he had to do that falling-in-a-tornado thing again.

Nope. The soles of his shoes hit solid rock. He was more worried about slipping. After walking several paces he had to climb. Big Mama let him do this himself, letting go and hovering over him while he felt around and climbed blindly, poking his feet and hands into whatever formidable slots and surfaces he could locate.

Up and up.

He spotted several room-sized caves in the rock, lit up dimly in yellowish light. Just before his arms and legs could get sore, Big Mama led him into one.

This one was wide, almost the size of his den. His wobbly legs stepped into it and it illuminated in blue, thanks to Big Mama thickening herself into a huge light tube, like a living, wiggly Glo-Stick. She drove him to a smooth jutting slab of rock that was almost as spacious as a bed. After a bit of trepidation, checking all around him, scrutinizing his every physical move, he sat.

A burning sensation hit his body. His hair felt like it was standing on end, and prickles up his skin. *Are those electric eels?* he thought weirdly. Dizziness swept into high tide. A fierce swoon threatened.

Big Mama hovered in front of him and gave him the circle. Jason returned it. A few more Big Mamas swam past his doorway.

His head felt heavy. His body felt drained of energy. Just as he was about to get comfortable, as comfortable as he could manage, someone or something appeared in the doorway.

He jerked back in alarm. He thought it was a monster, a little hunched thing with tentacles and a turned-over bucket for a head.

Nope, it wasn't a monster. It was his neighbor.

Ms. Millman.

"Well, hey there!" she said brightly, "Finally made it, huh?"

"I'm . . . "

He swallowed.

"I'm totally confused."

"There's no doubt about that."

She said something to the extent that he should take his time adjusting, that she knows he must be freaking out, just sit, don't worry . . .

He wanted to batter her with questions. There were so many things he needed to know.

He swallowed, unable to speak. She looked so ordinary standing there, her little handbag flung over her shoulder and her stylish little scarf around her neck.

"So I guess we're somewhere under the apartment complex?" was the first question he could muster.

"Yep. Pretty far below it. Its distance can only be measured until we hit that extra-dimensional portal. Then it's pretty much up to your imagination."

"I figured it was something like that."

"What does it feel like to you? Being here?"

"Ummm," he thought a second. "It feels like I'm spelunking in Hell basically."

"That's funny!" Her voice didn't signal that she thought it was. "This isn't hell though. Surely you don't think that."

"Not really. I guess I just don't have anything else to compare it to."

"It's merely where the Serpenteras live. It's like any other place where living things live. You just won't find it on a Rand-McNally map."

"Where the *whats* live?"

"What?"

"You said something about serpents, like some kind of name for them?"

"Oh . . . *Serpenteras*." She smiled. "I call them that. Do you like that word? *Serpenteras*? I made it up. It fits pretty well, I think."

He saw Big Mama float down in front of him. When she got close to his lap, her former body returned, the huge slug form he had first seen hanging out of his washing machine. She was heavy, but he tried not to let her know he was slightly uncomfortable.

Her head tilted back. The golden eye looked at him. He smiled at her and gave her the circle symbol.

Her body was vibrating. It reminded him of a cat purring. This wasn't a contented sound though. She looped herself around his torso.

She didn't seem too much like a slug any more, not real gooey or wet, just smooth and warm.

"Wow. It's great you guys hit it off!" Ms. Millman said. "I'm so glad. I was joking, of course, when I said you could kill them with salt. I'm not sure there is a way to kill them. Of course you really wouldn't want to."

"I almost did. Sorry."

"You were confused. You probably still are. It's understandable. She nodded towards Big Mama. "She's worried about her babies. They've gotten into some trouble lately." She gave him a knowing smile. "Impetuous youth."

She knew about the Carlos incident.

"My ex-roommate," he started. "They, um . . . "

"I know. They were just protecting their home like anything else would. Sorry about that guy. I really hope you weren't great friends."

"Not really. He brought it on himself, pretty much."

He just shrugged.

"I helped with the situation. I coached Big Mama to drive the car to an empty parking lot for a while. She got lost driving back. God, she was going to drive it back to your house after work!"

"Really?"

"Yes, they drove off the road into that house. One hell of a commotion around there, huh? Some of the baby Serpenteras are still missing. At this stage of their development they could die easily. She's worried."

He nodded, pretending to care. *Not my concern.*

Secretly, he knew his life would be a lot easier if they were dead. Mum's the word on that, for sure.

"Hopefully they will find their way back to your place, like the instinct a cat has. But it's very uncertain. They are kind of a new breed, let's say, Serpenteras adapted for land, a hybrid of earthen and, well, Serpentera life.

"They are evolving. I've been helping them with that. God knows it took me a long time to figure them out. I've helped guide their progress for the last twenty years. I can communicate with them but I'm not perfect. There's quite a bit of confusion and miscommunication between us. Lots, in fact." The giddy tone in her voice faded out. It was purely instructional now.

"Many are becoming earthen, developing into hybrid land and below land creatures, hence why they have to eat rotten flesh and vegetation. They don't eat humans or large animals. But this is an experimental stage, you know."

He shrugged. *Just keep talking. I'm too out of my depths to contribute.*

"I was the one who boarded up the windows in the building. I didn't board up yours so I could use my washer for my own clothes. Why the Serpenteras like to curl up in washing machines is beyond me. My own Serpy does that too."

She jerked a thumb over her head. One hovered there. It was a strange bluish color, thicker, pulsating more than Big Mama did.

"I guess, they like that fresh, clean smell. I always open

my window after I finish a wash. He comes in on cue every time."

"Weird," was all he could say. Now he wanted to ask her a question that was a little more down to earth.

"So, you own the building, not Mike?"

"No, it's Mike's. I'd buy it if I had the money. We have a deal worked out."

"What kind of deal?"

"He lets me live there and basically run it. He lives way out in the sticks, so he can't keep an eye on the property. He wants me to make sure it doesn't turn into a crack house. Which happens sometimes and I don't tell him. I let homeless people live there as long as they aren't dangerous. I did anyway, not as much lately with all the new tenants. It was just me and one other guy living there for a while."

She sighed. "He would rather not entrust me with it. We don't like each other very much."

"Wow." He pondered. "It's amazing you're allowed to stay there."

"Well, it does help that he's scared to death of me."

"How so?"

"He knows all about the Serpenteras. He thinks I'm witch. My baby transformed right in front of him several times. Once or twice he threatened to evict me. I sent my Serpentera to wreak havoc on him. Just little things. Just enough to send a message. Actually I'm part Serpentera. I can do this crazy thing with my eyes but I'm too ragged out to do it right now."

"Yeah, give me a rain check on that."

He heard something, from far off. Like a scream, maybe.

"This is a new stage of my life. I'm not getting any younger. I'm part of this new breed, all by myself" She laughed. "One of the perks is that I'm immortal. Or I'll be immortal when I'm complete."

"Complete?"

"I'm only halfway there. I'm taking it slow. I still have time to back out but I won't. One day . . . I'll take the jump."

"Immortality is pretty tempting, I guess."

"If I get there. I guess I'll have to wait and find out. I'm certain the offer will be extended to you, too. You've got the key to it all cuddled up on your lap."

"I'll have to pass on that, at least for the moment."

He had been hearing something, some distant spooky howling noise. During the pause, the sound got clearer. Its seemed to be a human voice, but his imagination could have been playing tricks. It certainly was coming from far away, somewhere else in the cavern.

Ms. Millman chuckled, knowing kind of chuckle, a tad sinister.

"Where's that coming from?" he asked. "God, that's freaky!"

Ms. Millman smiled slyly. "Much *much* farther down. Listen, Jason. Listen real good."

It *was* a human voice shouting.

"Who is that?"

"Take a wild guess."

It was impossible to determine. People screaming all sound alike.

"Is it Roger?"

"Bingo! I didn't want to break this on you so soon. We also have Carlos and some yuppie-looking guy and a policeman. We'll teach them some manners."

"Hey, you know, maybe that's a bit harsh, huh?"

"I'm kidding. I know having slaves probably isn't your style. Truthfully, their souls were diverted down here because the Serpenteras took the life from them."

"Ghosts? Good lord!"

"This is a new sort of thing down here. It's never happened before. I'm just as unsettled as you are about it. The good thing is that the Serpenteras that took their lives are still alive. They made it back down and deposited the souls here. But that does lead to other complications."

"How could it be more complicated?"

"The new breed of Serpenteras might have the ability to squeeze the souls out of their victims and take over their bodies. The fact that they deposited their souls here makes me concerned there is some kind of scheme going."

This statement was punctuated by another agonized howl from down below.

"I guess I know what you meant by *complications*. Are you sure this isn't Hell?"

"We don't do Hell things here. None of the boys down there are in any pain. They're just confused, the poor things."

Big Mama drifted up into the air and floated out the door. It was quite a sight to see her floating in her large physical form. In the light she looked like a glassy neon eel.

"Well, take some time and stretch out in your new place. It's nicer than our old place don't you think?

"Du-uh!"

Ms. Millman checked her watch.

"I have to get going. I need to check on the situation above ground. Then I need to check with the Serpentera council and get to the bottom of all this shit. What a day."

Jason noticed a cluster of Serpenteras were gathering around the doorway for some reason. He saw leaves and flowers lying on their backs as they floated.

"Now isn't that sweet! They're going to fix a bed for you. We'd better step out and let them get to work. C'mon."

She beckoned him forward. They stepped out of the cavern, back to where the flat rock staircases were.

"So just hang out here. I'll pop over in a little while. I'll pick you up some dinner. What do you like?"

"I'm not picky. I usually eat a lot of Chinese food. I practically live off of Willie Chan's. I like the orange chicken."

"Fine. The Serpenteras will probably offer you something. You can choose to eat it or not. It's bound to be interesting, but if you can handle Willie Chan's, then you have a pretty tough stomach."

Ms. Millman started descending the steps. She stopped again.

"And if you have to go to the bathroom: make sure you check to see if it's alive. Catch you later."

She stepped out of the cave.

Another apartment, he thought, two different apartments in one month.

He sat down on the cool slick rock. He could have been at peace, except for Roger's pathetic screams somewhere down in the caverns below.

*Pipe down, ya big baby. Don't make me mad. I might renege on my No Slave Policy.*

He peered over, trying to peer between what seemed miles and miles or smooth slick rock, a few jutting, what could be stalagmites, except they were curvy like crude S's, some shaped as pointed spirals jutting upwards in the murky gloom.

His curiosity was winning out over his fear. An urge struck him to climb down and explore. It could possibly be dangerous though.

He thought and looked over his shoulder at the swarming, fluttering Serpenteras fixing his bed. They were almost finished.

*I'll stay put.*

He fished a quarter out of his pocket and dropped it over. He heard nothing. He tried another coin but still heard nothing. Next he tried a whole handful of coins and hurled them down. He might have heard one or two dings. He was hoping he'd hear one of the coins hit the bottom.

There quite possibly wasn't one.

Later on, Jason fell asleep in the cave with Big Mama on his lap. He had been staring at her little golden eye pulsating in the darkness then ZAP . . . he was dead asleep.

*Did you knock me out, Big Mama?*

Only two or three more howls by the damned souls at the bottom then silence.

He awoke sometime later, then exhaustion took him like a swoon. His body felt heavy from the coma-like sleep he had been in, his head as heavy as a ceramic flower pot.

Groggily he wondered where he was, if he was still dreaming.

He remembered. He had to tell himself that he was merely underground, that his apartment was still overhead. Kind of.

It was just one dimension away.

*It's like camping,* he tried to tell himself.

Would he be able to get out? If so, how? He couldn't remember the route down here. What if something happened to Ms. Millman? Sure, Big Mama would help him, but they might not understand each other. An accident could happen. He could get clumsy, slip, and tumble into the abyss below.

Luckily his physical exhaustion pulled him back into sleep, his worries quelled by quiet mental darkness.

Two small Serpenteras glided up to him and nudged him awake. The little guys offered him some food: some dank rotted leaves and dead dried worms resting on their backs. He just smiled and shook his head.

Drowsiness washed over him, feeling a tickle in his stomach as if on a roller coaster ride, a roller coaster with no roller coaster car. He was hang-gliding in fierce winds. This sensation almost shook him awake. but sleep held a firm grip.

Maybe the Serpenteras offering the food spurred the weird dream, the dream of Roger and Carlos, sitting there with plates hovering over their round bulging bellies. Their forks stabbed vigorously into the mounds of thick Serpenteras, little babies whose bodies wiggled like fish out of water before they were crammed into the wide chomping human mouths. Carlos and Roger chewed wetly and crudely on the creatures before slurping them down. Their eyes were bloodshot and deadly.

Jason kept his eyes mostly on their bellies. Every time they swallowed one, their tummies would expand like balloons. Buttons on their shirts popped, and belly buttons became exposed. Carlos's was covered in hair, a big hairy belly Jason had seen way too many times while living with him.

Slurp, slurp and their bellies widened.

Jason kept trying to warn them to stop eating, pointing at their bellies which would explode at any minute. They didn't listen. Carlos made a smart-assed remark, eating even faster in defiance. He was extra peeved with Jason. This wasn't like the time Jason left his socks on the couch, the time he used one of his fancy plates, or the time he ate Carlos's cereal.

This time Carlos's touchy pride was triggered because Jason had killed him. It was a real dickish thing to do. He got blood and slug mush on his thirty dollar Nike t-shirt.

Carlos mumbled something to this effect while he ate, no exact words could be made out.

He said something like, "Remember that time you ate the rest of my Frosted Flakes then tried to deny it? You're busted, son. You bet your sorry ass I'm gonna eat your sluglettes . . . "

Expanding balloon sounds. The worst part about it was that Jason's face was level with their tummies so when they blew . . .

That big policeman was there, too, the one that got a huge mouthful before Big Mama hauled him away. This guy was the biggest and scariest.

Slurp, slurp, slurp . . . The huge cop, his face bloated and blistered with death, eyed him angrily as he munchy-munched on his slug critters, his belly popping the buttons of his policeman shirt, a yellow maggot or two, or three, squirmed from his belly button as it swelled like a balloon.

*Oh boy, this was going to be a nasty one . . .*

He awoke to the sensation of Big Mama's smooth, somewhat cold tail gliding across his shoulders, hearing multiple screams from below, as if the three hungry people in his dream exploded and were now screaming in agony.

He went in and out of sleep for a while after that, stretched across the rock bed. It was Ms. Millman who put the final coffin nail in his slumber by poking him in the shoulder.

"All right, neighbor. It's time to get you out of here."

"Aw, gee, mom. Let me sleep in a little while longer."

"No time for jokes. Up."

She was standing there, looking a little tired, her huge purse on one shoulder, her other hand dangling a white carton of Chinese food. The smell was wonderful.

As soon as he zeroed in on her face, he was taken aback by the sight of weird gold rings encircling her irises, giving her an otherworldly alien look. He didn't say anything, just stared.

"What?" she said.

"Your eyes."

"Oh!" she laughed and started blinking. "I didn't realize I looked like that."

She giggled and blinked.

"I'm not used to another person seeing me with this half-Serpentera thing going on. Remember I told you I could do a thing with my eyes? Well, this is the thing. My eyes get like this when I've been communicating with them."

"Okay. I think I can get used to it."

All of his life he had heard about Hell, how Hell was this, Hell was that. In his current situation, anything could trigger a Hell suspicion.

"Stop staring like that. You look like an idiot. Let's go."

"Hang on, Ms. Glow-in-the-Dark. I'm not used to sleeping on a rock. Let me stretch."

"Be snappy with it. The natives are getting restless."

"And that means . . . "

She smiled and crinkled her face to force an articulation.

"The critters, the Serpenteras, are a bit, well, *disturbed.* It's not you mainly. It's the other guys."

"The screamers?"

"Exactly."

"I don't blame them."

"They communicated something with me. It's really great how they are improving their use of the English language. A group of Serpenteras amassed in a huge cluster and spelled out to me . . . "

She drew the letters in the air, reading them aloud as she did so.

"GO 6 GO 111 1," she repeated, a bit unsure.

"And that means . . . "

"Well, obviously go means leave but six . . . "

"That's me!"

The realization hit him all at once.

"That's the symbol I use with Big Mama."

She scrunched her face.

"With my snake girl."

He pointed into his lap where she was coiled. She still seemed confused. He showed her the hand symbol.

"Snake girl?"

She sounded offended by his derogatory term, giving him a long stare. "Oh, I see."

Jason wasn't concerned. He asked, "But why *Go One thousand three hundred and Eleven*?"

"No, not one thousand three hundred and eleven."

She redrew them. He saw that she put a little loop at the top.

"It has to symbolize the four screamers down there. You have to leave with them."

"Wow. Is that possible?"

"I guess so. They're really nervous, keep fluttering around me. They keep pointing to the cavern of the deep darkness. That's a real spooky cavern that creeps out even me.

"It's pretty obvious they are freaking out. One of the oldest ones was trying to communicate telepathically. I was able to make it out as 'Jason to the dark cavern, souls to the surface.' Their language kept breaking into my brain while I was driving. It was very distracting."

"They can be real pushy."

"No kidding."

Ms. Millman handed him the Chinese food.

"Should I carry this?"

"Sure. Maybe one of them likes Willie Chan's. I don't know what else to do with it. Let's boogie."

He stopped a second. A pang of doubt fluttered, thinking about climbing down there and facing a foursome of dead guys. Am I going to see a ghost for the first time? *I've always heard people talk about ghosts but damned if I've ever seen one.*

Ms. Millman stared at him.

"I can't believe what we're going to do, that's all," he said, "Dead people. Wow."

"Don't shit your pants, tough guy."

During the descent, he kept an eye on Ms. Millman who he couldn't see but could hear nervously breathing. Considering her age, he had to worry that she wasn't quite nimble enough to handle the gradually sloping rocks.

He was having a tough enough time, feeling around blindly, expecting to trip over something at any moment. She'd obviously taken this route before. After a few feet down, the air turned frigid. The ground seemed soft all of a sudden. It was like they had fallen into a hole without actually experiencing the feeling of falling. He giggled as he felt his stomach lift.

Jason got a mean jolt of vertigo, stumbling back onto a bumpy slab of rock. He cursed. He elbow slipped briefly into an opening in the rock behind him.

*Who knows what could be inside that.*

"Still back there, Jason?"

"Somewhere."

Her voice was just barely above a whisper. He was suspicious about why they were whispering.

She reached out and patted him on the shoulder. She was barely two feet ahead of him.

"Just keep walking straight. Keep your hands out to your sides if you feel like you're losing your sense of direction. This path is pretty flat and obstacle-free. Sorry I didn't bring a flashlight for you."

"Don't sweat it."

"I'll keep talking so you can know where I am. Just reach out and poke me if you think you're falling behind."

"Okay. I thought you said you were gonna keep talking. So talk."

"You're being cheeky."

"Tell me a story, mommy."

"We're going to have to turn sideways pretty soon to fit through an alley coming up. Get ready. Don't be scared."

"You wish."

"It's surprisingly clean around here. You don't have to worry about moss, vines, spider webs, or any buggy-wuggies."

"That's reassuring."

"There are some really cool rock formations down here, columns and swirly things. Too bad you can't see them with your regular human eyes. With my Serpentera vision I can take it all in."

"Oh, no. This is quite lovely. This is the most beautiful pitch darkness I've ever experienced."

Sandra Millman chuckled at this. He reached forward and looped his finger around her purse strap just to make sure he was still heading straight.

He hated such unyielding darkness. He wanted to ask how far away from the pit they were, that bottomless abyss in the middle. His right hand was cramping from carrying the Willie Chan's carton. He shouted "Geronimoooo!" and flung it into the air, trying to reach the abyss part.

The food carton sailed a pretty good while and made a dull thump. Somewhere down there, probably on a jutting rock. The distance was still impossible to tell. The darkness was like a tremendous vacuum on his senses, rendering them useless.

Ms. Millman hissed at him in rebuke, "You . . . !"

"Sorry."

"You like people littering in your house?"

"Okay. Don't have a cow. It was merely a lapse in judgment."

He was lagging behind. Ms. Millman tugged at his shirtsleeve, pulling him forward.

"Turn sideways now."

He placed his palms against the rock in front of him as they inched along. Sandra gave him second by second updates on how much further they had to go.

"Just two feet now. Almost there."

The rock sliding across his back and fingertips felt too smooth to be rock. Not much friction. His back was beginning to cramp right as Ms. Millman announced they were at the end of the rock crevice.

They had arrived. The cavern of the deep darkness.

A haunted cavern. Spookville.

An undulating blanket of gray met them on that side, a shimmering oblong slit about the size of a window, thickening and receding before his eyes. Its distance was impossible to tell. One second it looked far away then a second later it appeared to be just a few feet in front of him.

"That's them?"

"Yep. Our buddies are waiting."

Ms. Millman made a weird noise with her throat, some bizarre sounds, maybe a poor attempt at Serpentera-speak. The language was like English played backwards and slowed down. Nothing happened. She sighed beside him and tried again.

Still nothing.

"I guess they don't know Serpentera-ese."

Total silence. She pulled him forward towards the ghostly wavering thing. As they got closer, it broke into strands, mixing in the darkness.

"I see them now."

"I can't see shit."

The misty grayness was growing thicker around them. It was harmless though, not harsh like smoke or damp like mist.

Just *there.*

"Hey." She said with a soft voice, nudging him. "Say something. They're close by."

"Who's close by?"

"The scr—"

As if to finish her sentence, four hell-stricken screams erupted around him. Great painful noise explosions blasted through him.

"Jason! Call for Roger. Damn it, boy! Grow a pair."

"Roger! Hey! It's your favorite lackey, Jason. Remember me from the retail slavery days?"

Nothing. Maybe the ghost-Roger was thinking, his former retail existence oozing back into his fractured memory.

*Maybe your life was too dull to remember, Rog.*

Ms. Millman slammed him with her elbow. She whispered, "Louder."

"Yo! Jerkwad!"

A cold hand gripped his forearm.

A *coldness* gripped his arm, coldness personified. A hand might not be involved.

The icy blast shot through Jason's entire body. It started clawing at his shirtsleeve, confusion and terror an invisible force in the pitch blackness.

He swiped at it, not really sure how to defend himself.

Ms. Millman was saying, "He's right on your left, don't touch him, I mean, don't stick your arm out too far . . . "

*Am I being possessed? Is this what being possessed by a demon feels like?*

*Just don't make my head start spinning around.*

He could feel the freezing death emanating from him. Or maybe it was pain, fear, or whatever kind of emotions spirits were capable of. A dead person was just a shapeless cloud of emotions, emotions all trying to jam through the same doorway at one time like the Three Stooges, then poking each other in the eyes, bopping each other on the head, and screaming in terror.

Or maybe . . .

They felt like a cold live person who was invisible and on fire, trying to extinguish itself by flailing around.

If pressed on the issue, that's how Jason would describe it to Dave and Chris at the Urban Turban one night.

"Well, here Roger, the human popsicle. What about the rest of the spook squad?"

"Spook what? Talk normal."

"The damn *screamers,* honey. Keep up."

"I think they are close by. I wish I had the foresight to bring a flashlight. Ah-ha!"

He could hear her digging around in her purse.

"My keys have a tiny flashlight on them. Hang tight. Don't you guys start getting romantic."

"Just find the fucking thing."

The keychain light was surprisingly bright for such a small object. Roger's wide scared eyes stared back at them in the grayish glow.

*Just ole Roger, the ultra-smug retail manager from Hell.*

Literally.

She swung the tiny light around revealing other faces in the inky darkness: the thick-necked police officer and buff lantern-jawed sports car guy. Carlos was in the back, the shortest one of all. Jason only caught a quick glimpse of them, their eyes were all wide as saucers, their faces stony and transfixed. Just the kind of expression he'd expect from three dead bastards.

Their looks were hazy, trapped in a body cast of drifting gray smoke. Their mouths were open poised in screams, the smoke-mist drifting into the gaping pit of their mouths. Wide-eyed Roger seemed to be sucking in the most smoke, panting in the dark hole with his mix-matched buddies.

Their mouths were pulled back at the corners, such to the extent it looked like an ice cream bar could easily be inserted into their mouths sideways.

Jason cleared his throat.

"Greetings. I am Jason of Earth. I have come to set you free. Except for Carlos. He has to stay. Just kidding, man. Seriously though. That dude died over a fucking can opener. He could have swung by Target and plopped down 2.95 for a new one, but *oh no,* he had to make a big deal of it. What a friggin' dork! Let's see a show of hands. Who wants to leave him here?"

"Hilarious, Jason. Really."

"Just trying to lighten the mood. Now what?"

"He's reaching out to you. Just kind of . . . stick out your elbow out to him. Carefully. Then, slowly ease back. He should latch on. If he goes with you the rest of him should follow. Let's hope so."

"All right."

Jason turned away and offered the crook of his arm to one of them. Coldness slithered around it. Belabored moans behind him. He stepped forward, sliding his feet to make sure the ground wouldn't trip him up. As he edged forward, Sandra said they were all following him.

"Keep it up. You're doing great. We have to turn sideways again soon."

Roger was still clinging to his arm as he slid into the narrow spot. He figured it was him since he was the skinniest one there. Roger seemed to resist a bit, pulling him back or maybe it was because he was heavy. He never knew a ghost could have any weight at all.

They started walking.

"Don't fall behind, Rog, you wimp. I just might to write you up for that! Going fast enough for you, sports car guy? You're a busy man, I know. Be careful of that cop behind you. He's got a quota to make. He'll have you doing community service until you're eligible for Medicare. Hey cop-ghost! You owe me for pulling you out of Hell. You have to fix my speeding tickets from now on."

"Oh, Jason, my boy. You've got issues," Sandra said.

Inching slowly sideways, he kept his left eye shut so he

wouldn't have to see Roger or the others. This path was more complicated now, and Jason needed to concentrate on scuttling between the rocks.

Once free of the slit, they just had to walk then climb. He reached out and plucked Ms. Millman's purse strap again, making sure she was still in front of him.

"Hang on, Jason. We're almost there."

It was too dark to see, but he guessed it was a kind of daisy chain, each gray-faced zombie attached to the other like a group of elementary school kids at a class zoo trip.

When they made it back to the cave, Big Mama floated on the exterior, her thick eel body shuddering with excitement. Ms. Millman took a seat on the inside of the cave.

"I think your pet is going to show you the way out, like when you came down here. She basically told me that, or tried to. I'm guessing here. I still got a ways to go before I can fully understand their language. I'm terrible with foreign tongues. Two years of high school French and all I can say is 'Comment allez-vous, monsieur?'"

Jason still couldn't look at the ghosts yet. With his senses grounding themselves again, he became aware of how odd Roger's grip on his arm was. Its pressure faded in and out. Its coldness created the same effect, fading in and out, but in a pulsating kind of way.

"Now, Jason," her voice had an edge of seriousness to it now. She took off her small glasses and rubbed her eyes. "You take them up there yourself. They are your responsibility from here on out."

"Wonderful."

"I'll level with you. I don't know what's going to happen when you take them out there and turn them loose on the world. Like everything else in this harsh beautiful world, we just have to let things be free to interact with everything else without judgment of them. Hopefully natural forces will know how to deal with this."

She went on to inform him that she called his job and,

pretending to be his aunt, and told them he got into a tiny fender-bender and that he wouldn't be in the next day. He asked her the time, how long had he been there. She said several hours, maybe five. But time was different here.

She couldn't ascertain the exact time. Maybe it was around eight o' clock.

"All my electrical devices, cell phone, watch, most things run by a battery die in here. I'm surprised as hell the flashlight worked." she said. "It's hard to keep the exact time."

Jason scoured his brain for something else to ask her. Turning around, Roger's wavy grey face stared back at him, lines under his wide eyes, smoky shadows framing this ultimate symbol of terror.

It reminded Jason of a face he had seen on one of those religious tracts Jesus people passed out and stuck in various places to scare people back to Christ.

Howling tortured faces of the damned sketched out in crude drawings. The same went for the cop, sports car guy and Carlos, trailing in the back. Fearful wide-eyed faces.

Faces of the Damned.

Damn.

Jason said, "Let's go," as Big Mama floated down and surrounded his head and started pulling him forward. He didn't like the way she could commandeer his body like that; muscles locking, neck aching, the stiff robotic movement in his legs, although she seemed better at it this time, guiding him more easily, and not quite so herky-jerky.

The daisy chain commenced. At the top of their ascent, he experienced something he didn't remember experiencing while entering the secret cavern: a feeling of being squeezed, being rung like a dishrag, then pushed through a tight opening like a womb, then . . .

Sunlight.

The fading light of dusk surrounded him and cool air filled his lungs. The funky smell of the woods rushed his nostrils. He felt his feet give away and tumbled to the ground. Big Mama unwrapped from around his head. He could see again. He watched as the four spirits followed after him, howling in fearful protest.

Out of burning curiosity, he looked back at the ground where they had emerged. There was no hole there at all. He saw just a big weathered junk tire, solid earth, dried leaves and spider webs within it.

No entry without Serpentera clearance.

He got up and started bending his arms and legs. He swiped at dirt and leaves clinging to his pants.

"End of the line, boys. I hope it was as fun for you as . . . "

When he turned to look at them he found that they had already scattered into different directions, not wasting time, lumbering pathetically as grayish human shapes into the darkening evening. A grayish smudge inked skyward.

The cop spook was flying.

His car remained where he had left it, sticking halfway out into the road. The house where the excitement had been was silent, a dirty white tarp taped over the front where Carlos's car had crashed. Two cop cars were closer to the house. Things had calmed down. Jason didn't stare, not wanting to attract attention.

The dusk became darker and Jason realized his keys weren't in his pockets. He opened the door and used the cab light to hunt for them in the tall weeds.

His fingers swept up the metal lump about a foot from the door. He fired up the engine.

Or tried to. The engine chugged weakly but didn't catch. *Oh, boy.* It did this sometimes. Now was not a good time. It finally caught and he chugged his way out of the ditch.

***

He made it home.

He made a few phone calls, first to his friends. He even called Melanie from work because he knew questions about him were swirling around. He figured it was better to get it over with now instead of being bombarded the next day.

He wanted to talk to people. He wanted to hear some human voices to ground him back into reality, at least a previous version that didn't include all the latest renovations.

He told everyone he was okay, trying to work within the narrative of being in a car accident. Dave and Jill were laid back about it but Melissa was a bit intense, still shocked about Roger's quick demise in the break room. She kept asking him if he was *sure* he was okay as if they had all narrowly escaped danger. She was a drama queen.

Janet, one of his supervisors, had a kind of sage-like disposition which probably came from mothering a huge litter of children.

*As long as you're okay, come on in tomorrow. It's cool.*

He told her he would.

After powering off his phone, he showered and ate. He had been in the cavern for about six hours.

It had felt so much longer. How weird.

# CHAPTER 6

THE NEXT DAY was an afternoon shift. The first hour of it was fine, reality firmly back in place. He had a feeling like he imagined an earthquake victim might have: a Richter scale rocker rumbles through your house knocking everything off the walls, off shelves, off tables, things broken, things scattered. Then you put everything back into its proper places, sweep up the busted stuff, rearrange the furniture and you feel normal again.

Work was like that for an hour.

Then, Roger staggered into the store.

Not the ghost Roger but the flesh and blood Roger that had choked to death in the break room the day before. He was even wearing the same clothes: a white button up shirt, tan trousers, except now they were smeared with dirt, some blood splotches on the front of his shirt and down his shoulder. His shoes flopped around his feet, laces dragging. It was a wonder security didn't block him from entering.

There were gasps all around.

"Roger?"

He just gazed around looking confused, out of his head. He locked his crazy eyes with Jason for a few seconds, standing next to the bargain rack.

"Oh, my God," someone else said.

Jason averted his eyes. Janet gave a *wait a second, please* hand motion to a customer she was helping, then sprinted up to him.

"Roger, w-we thought you died!"

"I died?"

"Yes!"

"Really?"

He was pathetically lost about what he was doing. Most creepy of all, he kept trying to make eye contact with Jason, as if he secretly knew Jason held the key to this.

Employees circled around him, peppering him with questions. Roger panicked and started breathing heavily. "Leave me alone! I just want to work. I'm not dead. Jason, tell them I'm not dead!"

"You're not dead, Roger," Jason said, offering a bit of sympathy. "You don't look great though."

At the center of the Book Barn there came a somewhat still, nervous commotion of furrowed brows and head shaking. Customers were becoming impatient, bordering on pissy. The check-out line had screeched to a halt. An old lady with paperback romance novels and some decorative laminated bookmarks huffed and started complaining.

Wendy, the part-time mother of two, newly hired, explained to her that Roger had supposedly died two days before, right in the break room, tittering as she asked the woman if she had a discount membership.

"I woke up in a morgue!" shouted Roger to the crowd, "A real goddamn hospital morgue downtown! Really!"

Jason noticed that Roger's speech was a bit slurred, like his jaw had been shot up with Novocain.

"Can you help me find a book?" said a customer, looking annoyed. Jason said sure.

Luckily the book the man sought was a common business book that they kept stacks of: *Seven Habits of Highly Successful People* by Stephan Covey. Even in his distracted state, he cruised right to it, whisking it off the shelf as Janet and Bill, the other manager on duty, walked Roger down the center aisle.

*I don't know what's going to happen when you take them out there and turn them loose on the world,* Ms. Millman had said.

Who would have thought they would want to return to their mundane earthly existences? His head expanded with these deep questions while Celine Dion's latest album lilted from speakers overhead, cash registers chimed, and small talk bubbled from customers.

Did this mean there was no afterlife? Or that the afterlife was worse than this? Roger could have soared to anywhere in the world but he wanted to come back to the Book Barn.

Maybe it was just because he was an idiot.

"Where's the cookbook section?" came a question beside him. "I'm looking for Rachel Ray's newest one."

Jason tried not to look angry. These questions needed to be resolved. Deep questions of much more heavy portent than a yuppie with a designer handbag could understand. Work was work though.

"Follow me, ma'am."

They were back there for about twenty minutes when Janet's voice came over the speaker system, "Jason to the main office, please."

They were in the store manager's office: Janet, Bill and Roger. Roger was sitting down in the swivel chair at the big desk, cutesy pictures of his kids in little free-standing frames all around him, a little teddy bear wearing a hat, fake flowers, and an opened box of Godiva chocolates. Roger was looking wide-eyed and jittery; his white button-down shirt lined with blood, possibly mucus, and dirt streaked everywhere.

*And let us not forget the blob of pus leaking from one of his gray eyeballs.*

*Ew.*

Bill kept telling him to calm down, and kept asking him to go home: *Take a break, man. Get some rest. We can't have you on the floor acting like this . . .*

"What do you know about his condition?" Janet asked

Jason. If she was Caucasian, not black, she would have been white as a ghost.

"I know nothing, absolutely nothing. How should I? I left before everything went down yesterday."

Play dumb. *The truth is beyond your comprehension, Janet.*

"He keeps asking for you."

Jason shrugged.

Lowering her voice a notch, "He just keeps saying that you know he's not dead. *I'm not dead. I just want to work.* The boy is out of his mind."

Roger was waving his hand at him.

"I'll stay here and help Jason with his section. His section is a mess, right, Jason? I'll help him."

At the word *help* Janet jerked back. While speaking certain words, Roger would douse the air with a disgusting pinkish spittle that would then go on to trickle down his lips and chin.

The expression, *say it don't spray it,* was never more appropriate.

"You are *not* going out on the sales floor," ordered Bill. "You're raving like a maniac, you've got blood on your shirt, dirt everywhere . . . C'mon. Get serious."

"Lori is in the women's room," said Janet to Jason, referring to the store manager. "The poor girl got sick. I can't blame her."

What she most likely got sick from, which was grossing them all out, was the brown crusted blood going from Roger's left ear to his neck. More crusted blood was inside of his ear. They were all trying not to look at it. Bill was holding a wad of wet paper towels. They didn't say it but they all wanted to clean that ear off.

"Your ear, Roger," Bill finally said. "Your ear is really . . . Can you hear okay?"

"Yes," said Roger. "Here is okay."

"No, I mean your ear . . . "

The ear drum was definitely shattered. By what . . . who knows? Roger was just going to stammer, look around and repeat the same thing anyway.

"I just want to work."

A police officer kept peeking in. Lori was consulting with him outside. He had a gun, taser, the whole deal, and looked ready to use it at the least provocation.

Jason had seen news stories about policemen tasering the shit out of people for no reason, just because they acted a tad erratic.

*That's all I need. He died and was brought back to this pathetic condition because of me and now I get to see him tortured with an electrical device. Not cool.*

Janet nudged him on the arm. *Say something. Help us with this nutcase.*

"What Bill is saying, Roger . . . " began Jason, "is that you can't work tonight. You've had an accident. You need time to recover."

Janet nodded approvingly.

"But that doesn't mean you can't come back to your normal job. Everything's cool."

"Yeah," said Bill nodding. "Everything's fine, Roger."

"Absolutely," said Janet.

"But you're in no shape to work right now. They won't mind if you hang out here tonight. Just stay in the back, until you feel better."

He glanced around at Janet and Bill. They shrugged, nodded.

"Sure, it's no problem," Bill said, although he didn't look enthusiastic about it.

"He doesn't want to go home," said Jason to Bill and Janet. "He didn't have a wife or any serious significant other that we knew of, right?"

They nodded. Janet added that he had a girlfriend, but she couldn't think of her name.

"I don't think he had a particularly satisfying home-life

which is why he decided to come here. This is the only real life he had, his only purpose."

They nodded along. Jason suddenly realized he shouldn't continue to refer to Roger in the past tense.

"Let him stay here. Call his girlfriend, mom or whoever cares the most about him. If nothing else, I'll, or *we'll,* take him home after we close. You should let him chill out here for a while."

"I guess there ain't nothing else to do," said Janet.

"I'll get the security guy to keep an eye on him." Bill said, grimacing. Roger did smell bad.

"Thanks a lot, Jason." Janet patted his shoulder, "You did a good job. Get on back out there. The floor's probably going nuts."

Bill nodded too, as if to half-heartedly concur with her sentiments. Jason hurried out.

Roger's girlfriend showed up later. Jason recognized her as someone who hung out at the store, usually sitting at a table near the window sipping on a paper cup of coffee, not interested in much else besides interior design magazines and book-of-the-months from the shelves. Like most customers, she probably never put them back. She seemed slightly uppity, but not too much, her clothes tasteful, but not too sleek or fashionable: a jeans and blouse kind of gal. She had light brown hair and was pale, with a nearly lipless mouth.

She didn't act like she wanted to be there and didn't have any luck pulling Roger from the back, like the other managers had hoped. Bill discussed the situation with a group of concerned police officers. Things could have heated up, but Bill managed to defuse the situation.

There were still one or two police officers and security personnel milling around when they closed the store.

It took forever to coax Roger from the office. He kept clinging to Jason as they walked him from the back, lumbering along beside him, talking gibberish in his lazy slack mouth manner, drool cruising down his chin. He was saying something about his iPad then started sputtering some words Jason realized were lyrics to a Simon and Garfunkle song. "Me and Julio Down by the Schoolyard".

It was like dealing with a bad drunk, except there was no hope that Roger would eventually pass out and spare everyone the agony. He became more animated as he walked along.

"Urr-meen guurn moin . . . "

His gibberish was like the sound of a phonograph record being played backwards. It seemed familiar.

Before they got to the glass door to the front entrance, Roger squeezed Jason's shoulder tight and muttered close to his ear, "I did good, right? Muurl-ee . . . I told them I wanted you to . . . to take my job. They'll like that, right? Really good they will like it, good and not send me to deep dark down."

"They who?"

"Pretties. Snakes. No dark cold. They will let me go when I die. No cave in cold dark."

The caverns.

"They will like what, Roger?"

"Meer-een . . . "

"The snakes sent you here to do something?"

"Oo-uh gurnin huugh!"

A chubby, but brawny cop, shook his head, looking at Jason, keeping a keen eye on him and a hand on his taser.

Outside in the parking lot, they practically had to cram Roger into his girlfriend's Volkswagen. Jason never left his side. Once in the car, Roger kept his foot against the door so they couldn't shut it, just blubbering nonsense to Jason.

The door shut finally. No word of thanks from the mousey girlfriend, just embarrassment and disgust at her situation. Janet thanked Jason again. Bill just grunted and tiredly slouched to his car.

Jason drove home. He wanted to tell Sandra about what happened but her light was out. He tried knocking, but got nothing. Exhausted and wanting to put everything behind him for the day, he scribbled a quick note about what happened with Roger and wedged it in her front door.

He went up to his room and stretched out on the bed. He wanted to sleep, but stretching out in a quiet apartment was good enough for a while.

***

That was the last Roger would see of the Book Barn. The stunning miracle of returning from the dead merely extended his life another two days. His brain quickly deteriorated and he passed away around seven o'clock the next morning.

Janet called him and told him. She also asked for him to come in a few minutes early because she had something with him to discuss.

This was no easy task. He was working a mid-shift which meant he had to clock in at eleven. He had worked a late shift the night before. He barely got three hours of sleep.

***

At work, Jason huffed through the door merely five minutes early. Janet smiled as she walked up to him.

She led him into the office and informed him of Roger solemnly. She also made certain to let Jason know how much she appreciated his help.

"I know nobody thanked you," she rolled her eyes. "Bill is just Bill and Judy was all huffy. Despite all that, I want you to know you did a big thing and you were under a lot of stress I know."

"All in a day's work."

"That's a good way to look at it. Speaking of work, there is something else on my mind. Through all of his jibber-jabber, Roger told us a few times that he wanted you to take his place as manager. He said he just wanted to shelve books and magazines and wanted you to take his place."

She laughed.

"I know he said a lot of things that were zany, but that made sense. You've been working here quite a while and you have a good deal of retail experience."

"Am I on good terms? I was thinking not."

"Sure, you are! Personalities clash but you're a solid worker. Everybody knows that."

"I find that hard to believe."

"Everybody is under pressure here. We've got product to move and expectations to meet, so there's no time to coddle everybody's ego. That's the way it is."

"What about the write-ups? One more and I would have been fired."

"Those are debatable. I don't think you really did anything wrong, as far as I can remember. You stayed on break too long once? Like a minute or two?"

"Barely that. Roger was being a real butthead."

"And the first time . . . "

"I fell asleep in the break room."

Janet cackled and clapped her hands.

"You deserved that one! Well, you show up on time, you're diligent and you're a darn good bookseller. The best one we've got."

"Are you sure the write-ups aren't a big deal?"

"Honey, they're just sitting in a folder in the office. Roger might have been the only person who knew about them or could remember you had them. But still, they're excusable, I won't mention them. I'll do some sneaky Jedi Mind-Trick so the issue doesn't come up.

"The hard part will be to convince the others to go along. They might say you're too young, that you don't have enough experience or, you know, something else might bump up against their egos. I can't guarantee it but I will do everything to push this through. I'm gonna push real hard for you."

"Thank you, Janet. That would be a great opportunity for me. Manager. Wow."

"You deserve it. See you Sunday. We'll talk more then. You are working Sunday, right?"

"Yep."

"Bye. Thanks again."

Jason left the office, fishing his nametag out of his pants pocket. By the magazine shelves, Melanie was engaged in a spirited conversation with a tall-ish blond girl with short cropped hair. Jason thought he could escape. Too late. Mel flapped her chubby hands in his direction. He cruised over to her.

"Oh, Jason, this is my roommate! Her birthday's on Saturday. Remember?"

"Well, sure."

"Didn't think so. This is probably the tenth party I've tried to drag him out to."

She winked to her roommate.

"Jason thinks he's too good for us!"

"Whoa, hey, that's pretty harsh. Your timing has just been bad."

He *was* avoiding her parties. Any sane person would. About twice a month she liked to throw a movie-themed party. She usually announced them on the break room corkboard, adorned with crudely drawn kitties and smiley faces: Matrix Marathon at Melanie's! Star Trek Marathon this Friday at Melanie's! Babylon 5 Marathon at Melanie's! Sodas, cookies, and **craziness**!

Nerd central. He was basically cool with nerds, perhaps a variation of one himself. He was a more brooding aloof kind, not the herd-mentality "Trekkie" types like Melanie and her ilk.

Staring at her exquisite roommate changed everything. Her eyes were so big and sparkly, he could have fallen in. He would have gladly.

She was magnetic. Jason immediately started questioning her. Her name was Julia, an art major at Georgia State, a sophomore. Jason mentioned he had been a student there, but currently was on hiatus. What a lie.

Not only was this girl nearly the spitting image of his ex, Jill, but she was exuded quality, that perfect posture that oozed a gentle confidence, the way she cocked her head and smiled brightly which told him she actually cared about what he was saying.

She was just turning twenty one.

"The magic age!" he said. "You're old enough to drink now."

"I'm old enough to do a lot of things."

*Was that a pass at me?* A little smirk flashed after that, right as she turned away.

"See you at the party," he said, not sure if she heard him.

"I'm will hold you to that," she said, turning around and shaking her finger, a sexy lilt in her voice.

Melanie giggled and said something he didn't catch. From the customer service desk, Bill summoned him. Jason said, "Wait," then staggered to the back to clock in. One of the part-timers surprised him by saying "Hi" to him. He got a "What's up, Jason?" from another part-timer shelving the True Crime section.

That was new. Usually, he felt invisible at work.

The word MANAGER kept flashing in his head. A few extra bucks an hour would be just the ticket. Plus a manager position would be well-deserved payment for being on the bottom so long. A bottom populated by mental midgets who seemed to have gained their supervisory positions from sheer luck and nothing else.

*What does it take*, he always asked himself *to move up in a job?* From his experience, you were treated like a lackey no matter how hard you worked. Working too hard, dedicating yourself to a position just multiplied your resentment when they eventually screwed you over.

So many times, he watched his managers in a circle chatting and laughing while he yanked loaded dollies around, scuttled about checking for books, tagging and inventorying. It seemed like such a sham.

Working hard didn't mean squat. It was all luck.

Maybe this would be his chance, his big break into the elite world of retail management. Something dignified to toil at until he discovered his real career.

The store manager trotted by and greeted him as he

heading up the center aisle. Even big surly Bill, the floor manager for the afternoon, gave him a "How-ya-doin-Jason" at the Customer Service desk while checking the computer for a customer.

When things slowed down a bit, Bill engaged him in a little light-hearted conversation about some celebrity on *Dancing with the Stars* the night before. Jason played along, smiling and chuckling pretending he knew what Bill was talking about.

*Nice try, Bill. We still have nothing in common.*

He really did want to connect with Bill somehow. Bill was big into sports, baseball and football mainly. Sometimes, Bill asked Jason if he'd seen this game or that game. Jason always just shrugged, told him he knew zip about sports.

He was trying hard to think of something to talk about when a skinny dude, in a red and orange flannel shirt, bounded over one of the display tables with an armful of front-listed, top-of-the-line art books. The guy must have had rabbit feet. Even Olympic high jumpers needed a running start. He even managed to leap over the table without knocking down the 30% off sign.

"Holy sh—" spat Bill.

The portly store detective rounded the corner wide-eyed, huffing as the graceful thief tore through the double doors of the front entrance. There were a few startled shrieks from customers. One scruffy guy standing with his wife at in the check-out line hooted in laughter.

"I ain't never seen a crack head jump *that* high before!"

Jason shot him an offended stare.

Yes, there was a crack house down the street that unleashed thieves onto the retail community. Yes, the thief probably smoked crack. Yes, he jumped high in the process of his escape. How observant.

The store detective was on his walkie-talkie within seconds, alerting the outside security team, still out of breath. He was trying hard to maintain a cool composure.

*Good luck catching that guy.*

Then he spun around and eyed Bill. A manager huddle commenced in the most secluded corner of the store, the store dick quarterbacking it. Lori Driscoll, the store manager, tried to take charge. Jason had seen this unfold many times before.

Jason manned the customer service desk all by himself. Everybody had something to talk about now. All the other peons would be abuzz, talking about this for days.

Fun, fun, fun.

With all the managers tied up and one part-timer a no-show, they were shorthanded and he was extra busy. Phones rang virtually nonstop. A few customers wanted their books shipped. One customer got snippy and complained that Jason wasn't giving them enough attention. Two other full-timers showed up from the back.

They worked in overdrive. It still wasn't enough. Stray books piled up along the windows and on the tables. It would have been great to question Mel about her roommate: did she have a boyfriend, did she have an almost-boyfriend, was she on any anti-psychotic medication . . . relevant information.

But work was too hectic.

He even skipped his fifteen minute break.

It was inevitably gearing up to be another Urban Turban night. Chris had sent one of his notoriously garbled text messages about hanging out at the Turban. For once, Jason had a reason to celebrate. Hell, several reasons: the possible promotion and meeting a girl.

All in the same day.

For all his hard work, Bill still asked him to stay over thirty minutes. One of the part-timers was running late.

Part-timers were always late.

Jason begrudgingly agreed to work however long they needed him. It was almost eight o'clock before he finally extricated himself from that place.

***

In his car, Jason rolled down the window, a cool breeze flowing in. He popped in The Cramps on CD, the ancient blown speakers farting a kazoo-sounding accompaniment.

He cruised by Willie Chan's and picked up an orange chicken set meal. The food tasted so good and piping hot, he wasn't bothered by the long slow line he had to stand in at the counter in order to get it. Dave responded to his text and said he could probably stop by.

He also noticed that Ms. Millman had tried to call him twice. He made a mental note to get back with her later.

In the apartment, he took a few minutes to scope around for Big Mama. He really didn't want to see her, but he'd rather seek her out than be surprised by her later. She could suddenly whiz into the room as a spindle, peek around the corner, or even be clinging to the ceiling. He didn't like those kinds of surprises.

"I'm home, babe. Got a kiss for your favorite mammal?"

Nothing. He looked into the washing machine and, to his surprise saw that it was empty.

Not a sluppie to be found. All gone.

Now his list included three great things: a possible promotion, meeting a hot chick and *no more sluppies*!

What an amazing day.

***

Chris was at the bar in the main ballroom nursing a Pabst when Jason got there. The music was at mid-volume, the bar staff stocking up. Lotus waved and Jason waved back.

Chris appeared shocked when Jason ordered an imported beer.

"Getting all fancy these days, huh? A Red Stripe! Is that what you drink at the country club with your Harvard friends?"

"I'm celebrating."

"Don't name it after me."

Jason offered to buy him a fancy beer.

"No thanks. I don't want to spoil myself with that tasty stuff. So what are we celebrating?"

Jason told Chris about his possible promotion at the Book Barn. Chris congratulated him. Jason didn't mention the girl. She was way too speculative at this point. It was best not to jinx it anyway.

Jason went on to explain what happened to Roger, his near fatal choking accident, how he wandered back to work only to die two days later. Then he cheerfully described Janet pulling him aside saying how much everyone appreciated his hard work . . .

"Whoa, whoa. Back up. What happened to your manager again? The dude died then . . . what?"

Chris gave him an incredulous look. Jason went over it again.

"Are you sure you didn't bump him off? It's just so bizarre how you rattled all that off, like it was some everyday occurrence. It's just funny, you know?"

"Yeah, yeah. That put my week onto a freaky course."

"That's life though, I guess. People die every day. Cheers, my man."

They clinked beers. The place stayed pretty vacant for a while. They ordered some food and chatted up Lotus when he emerged from the back with his black apron around his shoulder. By the time Dave arrived, the club had started to fill up. He, too, remarked on Jason's fancy beers.

"We're mourning and celebrating at the same time," said Chris.

"So, Jason finally lost his virginity?"

"Ha ha."

"No, Jason killed off a co-worker and took his job."

"Intriguing," said Dave. "Tell me more."

Jason spilled it. He made sure to give the telling a more human angle this time, going slower.

"Is that freaky or what?" said Chris.

"Sounds like some kind of aneurism," contemplated

Dave. "I think I've heard of something like that in fact. Sometimes choking victims don't completely die. They can resuscitate easily. I guess the lack of oxygen damaged his brain, then the next day he . . . "

Dave gave up, flipped his hand.

"I don't know. It still sounds pretty *Outer Limits* to me."

They were each distracted a second watching Lotus and the bartender. Lotus had a tub full of cleans pint glasses and was tossing them to the bartender, all the way at the other end of the bar. The really weird thing was when the bartender started catching them from behind his back, without looking.

Even when Lotus tossed them short, the nimble barkeep dove forward, swooping them right up with ease. No glasses came close to hitting the floor.

"That must be some new act they're working on," remarked Dave.

"Some girly cocktail show? Let's pray it doesn't happen."

"Showing off like that is annoying."

The thin crowd whooped and applauded. They had never seen this bartender move so fast. Usually, he crept along the oval of the bar at a near sleepwalking pace. No matter how hard you stared him down, he would never hurry.

Suddenly he was some kind of acrobat?

"Oh-my-god, oh my god, ohmyGOD!" said Jason. He wrenched them by the shirtsleeves and shook them. He suddenly remembered the thief springing over the New Releases table. He zealously described every detail.

Dave and Chris exploded with laughter. Chris buried his head in the bar for about ten minutes. Dave made Jason describe it again. He did. Then Dave begged for even more details.

"It was a seriously expensive, cloth-bound, Edward Hopper photobook."

"Hopper!"

"The dude knew exactly which ones to get."

"Shut the fuck up!" begged Chris. "You're killing me, man!"

"Thieves in this town are just evolving, that's what it is," Dave explained. "Like ducks acquiring webbed feet to swim faster, giraffes growing long necks so they can reach high leaves. Petty criminals are acquiring springing ability so they can steal shit easier. Evolution is speeding up. I applaud this new stage of their development."

"He must do some hard core leg exercises," Jason mused. "The dude must have calves the size of Butterball turkeys!"

"No, no, no. Here it is."

Dave put on a look of dead seriousness.

"You should've looked at his feet. I *guarantee* you he was wearing some kind of special shoes. He probably designed them himself, made some shoes with springs in them, springs made out of some fuckin' NASA grade titanium or something. Thieves are clever motherfuckers, man."

Chris tossed his head back, laughing.

"You don't believe me, but I'm serious. These small time thieves have underground think tanks where they come up with this stuff."

"They are clever. Yet not clever enough to make a real living," said Chris.

"Make a living? Hell, if thieves poured a mere *fraction* of their creative energy into something beneficial to mankind, we'd be colonizing the moon already."

All three of them were in pain from laughing. More rounds were ordered, clinked, and guzzled.

Their merriment was short lived. Tonight was Goth Night at the Urban Turban. Their jocularity didn't mix well and was sufficiently quelled after three or four depressing songs.

They weren't planning a late night anyway. Chris and Dave had obligations in the morning; Dave had work, Chris had class.

They shuffled out to the parking lot. A crowd was gathered out there. At first Jason thought it might be a fight. Nope, people were cheering and clapping. A group of onlookers slid away and Jason saw something spinning.

Strange colored swirled within it. As his eyes adjusted, he figured out. It was a guy spinning on his head.

The purple scarves gave off this strange spiraling effect, seeming to thin out the faster he spun. He was like a human top. The crowd oh-ed and ah-ed, clapped hands, and whooped. As he slowed, Jason saw that he was spinning not on his head but on his finger.

Chris remarked about this just as Jason realized it.

Gracefully as possible, the spinner slowed enough, did a flip then landed on one toe, continuing his spinning but slower; one hand securing his other foot. He was smiling widely. Jason recognized his face but couldn't place him. Maybe it was the clothes...

As he came to a stop, his hand flung upward. From the cuff of his black coat emerged a live dove. As it spread its wings to take off from his palm, it faded and disappeared. The crowd went wild. From his other palm emerged a green and yellow parakeet. It tweeted right before it also disappeared.

More applause.

Jason, Dave and Chris stared at each other, mouths open, heads shaking.

As he bowed to the crowd, grinning and turning to everyone in attendance, Jason recognized him. It was The Magician from the diner, that weirdo who always looked so morose and immobile. Apparently, there had been quite a change in him; one hell of a change.

Jason strode up to him, gripped his hand and shook it vigorously. Jason told him how amazing his show was, said he had seen him around.

"Remember me from the diner?"

"Of course, man!"

"To tell you honestly, I was wondering about you. You always seemed kind of depressed. I was curious about what your deal was. You're on fire now though!"

He had to wait a second while others in the audience

came over and told him how amazing his act had been. The Magician thanked them. Some people plopped money in his upside down top hat.

"Yeah, man, thanks. It was a low point. I was just doing cheesy magic tricks, make this and that disappear. Let's just say I spiced up my act a bit."

"No kidding. How do you spin on your finger like that?"

"It's magic. I just do it, man!"

"And the birds," said Dave. "They looked real. How do you do that?"

"It's magic, baby!"

Jason saw that his top hat was held up to his chest. He fished around for some changes, bills. Dave and Chris tossed in something. As he was putting two bucks in, he was startled as a rabbit hopped onto his hand from within the hat. He could even feel it. Like the birds, it quickly faded and disintegrated into the air.

"How do you do that?"

The Magician flipped the hat over. Nothing fell out. His other hand emerged holding a bill with the face of Ulysses S. Grant.

"Got change for a fifty?" he asked, smiling.

Dave, Chris and Jason turned away and started through the parking lot, winding through the thick energetic crowd.

"It's got to be holograms or something," said Dave. "The technology available these days . . . "

"It's all the showmanship," said Chris. "That dude was pretty damn good. It was brilliant when he made that parakeet tweet."

Chris gave them a salute and veered off to where his car was parked. Dave soon did the same. Jason waved goodbye then stared back where the magician was.

He had started spinning again.

***

When he got into his apartment, he already started dreaming about the changes he would make to the place when he got his pay increase. A sofa, for God's sake, some pictures, a new stereo, an area rug, and maybe one of those artsy lamps from that store in mid-town.

He passed the lamp store on his way to work every day. Currently, its window displayed a huge silvery lamp shaped like an octopus. It probably cost several hundred bucks, maybe a thousand. He deserved something like that after living so Spartan.

*That octopus lamp is so mine.*

He snatched a duct-taped lawn chair from the corner of the room and imagined the octopus lamp there with his eight little lamp-shaded tentacles dancing out into the air.

*So totally bad-ass.*

Who needs a couch when you have an octopus lamp? He would have to get some kind of end table. He'd have to buy the end table first before the octopus lamp . . .

A *bang-bang-bang* emanated from the door. Not a regular knock. This one had lumberjack force behind it. *Bang-bang-bang-bang* . . . It was apparent that if he didn't open it, the person would just keep right on banging.

A huge barrel-chested black cop lurched in when Jason opened it. His face was banged up. His eyes were wide and crazy. The front of his filthy uniform was drenched in blood.

Jason jumped out of his way just in time to see him crash onto the floor. In his sinewy bloody drumstick of an arm, he gripped a bright red gym bag. Dark red fingers, the shattered remains of his hand, dropped pathetically; just an amorphous ball of meat.

The gym bag jutted out like a ridiculously large purse, bills poked out of the opening, some soaked in blood, some scattering across the floor.

The bag was stuffed with money. It was almost squashed by the huge corpse.

The cop was very, very dead.

Dead twice.

This was the same cop that had shouted at him right

before Big Mama whisked him away, that huge muscleman of a cop. He was one of the screamers.

Jason shut the door and stood over the dead man, transfixed by the sight. He scanned the guy's contorted face for movement. He noticed the eyes were still open in small dark slits.

He opened the door again and looked out. An unfamiliar car was parked in the middle of the road, its headlights on. A compact late-model hatchback with the passenger side door open, the cab light glowing dimly in the distance.

Jason rolled him over, grimacing at the sight of various bills sticking to his gory, bloody chest. There were about three bullet holes there.

*Real fucking bullet holes.*

Only an animated corpse could have survived long enough to drive in order to deliver this.

A gym bag full of money. Cash. Moola. Dead presidents.

This was another favor undoubtedly, from the "Pretties, the snakes."

He remembered Roger saying: *"They'll like that, right? Really good, they will like it good and not send me to deep dark down."*

If the cop had lived long enough he probably would have said something similar.

Where did it come from?

Who cares? He had a dead body in his den.

Again.

***

There was a sickening taste in Jason's mouth. *All that blood.* He hadn't seen so much blood since he was a little boy watching his dad skin a deer.

*Don't toy with my species. It's bad enough that you kill. You should at least let them rest in peace afterwards, not have them run around town doing errands.*

Running around doing errands. *Bad joke.* It didn't lighten the situation at all. This was serious business. This guy would start changing soon, going through stages dead bodies went through.

Jason checked the outside of the apartment; the same dark, lonely street. Nobody saw anything. The burn-out kids were probably too drunk or drugged up to be sharp with details anyway. When they weren't home, they stayed out late. The Goth chick had been AWOL for a while. He had noticed a Marilyn Manson look-alike frequenting her door these days. She was probably with him.

He got in to the car, drove it to the curb and shut off the engine. He was careful not to touch it too much. No fingerprints could linger. It was bad enough that a dead body was stinking up his apartment. It'd be worse to go to death row over it.

He hurried to Sandra's place and knocked on the door.

Brightly ringed eyes greeted him. He jumped back.

"Damn, boy, grow a spine, will ya? This happens when I communicate with them."

He pushed his way inside and shut the door behind him.

"That's great," He said, darting into the kitchen to wash his hands in the sink. At least she was wealthy enough to afford paper towels.

This was his first time in her apartment and he couldn't help being struck by the huge framed paintings on her walls. They were her work undoubtedly, colorful swirling thick shapes and curlicues all melded together: Serpentera art.

"Since you've been talking to them, you need to call them up. Rally the troops! I got a big bloody mission for them up in my apartment!"

"What?"

"Oh, you know, just another *dead body.* It's one of the screamers. They're all coming back to life. Briefly. They seem to be trying to do favors for me."

"A dead guy? *Dammit.* This is all I need!"

"I concur. Can they do him like they did Carlos? Make him drive away?"

"You're S.O.L this time, buddy. I mean, it's not like I have a special whistle to blow and summon them. I don't have a built-in honing device like Big Mama. Maybe they can sense our situation. You could get lucky, but you should plan to get rid of the body yourself. Big Mama is really upset."

"Super."

"A lot of the above ground Serpenteras are missing, the ones that attacked those people. They're just gone."

Sandra took a sip from the mug she was holding. Some kind of hot tea; a little baggie hung over the rim.

"Well, I can't be much help to her if I'm a murder suspect. I was assuming those critters could take care of themselves. You know, like they had inborn instincts or something."

"Me, too. It's just strange. It's like they just wandered off."

"That's for later, Sandra. Let's go upstairs. It's time to haul some meat."

Wearing only a silk Chinese robe, she needed another minute.

"Let me get dressed first, for God sake."

***

"Wow. He's a big fella."

She peered over the body. Sandra was wearing a pair of rubber dishwashing gloves. She had an extra pair for him.

"Impressive observation skills you have."

She made an excited sound at the sight of a tiny Serpentera creeping across the guy's cheek, slowly thickening into its slug-resembling shape. He was quite sure the thing hadn't been there before. He was positive of it.

*It had just crawled out of him.*

It did look gooey, leaving a faint trail of blood in its tiny path; a sickeningly stringy path that led from his ear.

There was more pulpy vileness around the dead body's ear. An unnatural looking hole was there. Jason ran to the kitchen. The *smell*. It was a faint rotting smell mixed possibly with shit. Roger had smelled like this too, but not quite as bad.

He returned with a can of Lysol. He coated the air with it.

Sandra tied a handkerchief around her mouth.

He asked her where the Serpentera went. She said it flew away, smiling, sighing.

"There were three actually."

"That's disgusting. In his *brain*?"

"Yep. It was great to see them take flight after that. It's amazing that they still have the power."

"Maybe because they had his soul."

"No. They won't mess with souls again. They weren't so happy with them last time."

"So, how should we do this? This isn't my field."

"It's not mine either. I'm thinking."

"Think faster."

"We'll have to chop him into little pieces I guess."

"Hell, no!"

"I'm kidding. It's not like some late night movie where a guy accidentally kills his wife. You have no connection to him. It's just a matter of taking his body somewhere and leaving it there."

"But where?"

"There are plenty of abandoned alleys around here. I've got a nice dank one in mind right now. It's about ten miles away, secluded, nothing around it. I'll take my car and scout it out. I'll make sure there are no roadblocks or anything around, then I'll come back and we'll take care of it."

"It can't be that simple."

"It has to be. We've got to get him out pronto. Just in case someone is pursuing him. You know, whoever he stole the money from."

"Let's get a move on then."

Sandra did just that. She returned twenty minutes later. While she was gone, Jason covered the body in trash bags and twisted strands of tape.

*This is so disrespectful.*

When she returned, Sandra informed him that he had wasted his time. "You've seen too many movies. Just walk him out there like you would a live person, like you're carrying a drunk. Trash bags are way over the top."

"Now is no time to nitpick."

"You should be more concerned with video cameras. Some traffic lights have them, some businesses have them. Our route has to avoid them, because the police will seriously be looking into this. That could be our fatal flaw."

"Good thinking."

They got on both sides of the cops and hoisted him up. The sour feces smell made an encore, its closing number.

*"This tune is called 'Shit and Bile Oozing from a Corpse', ladies and gents. Remember to tip your waitresses . . . "*

Even Sandra gagged. Taking the body downstairs was a hard trick but the gravity of the situation seemed to infuse Jason with more strength than he normally had. The rest was surprisingly easily.

They just left him sitting in a car.

Parked in a smelly underpass. The trash bags and tape were more dignified. Jason knew it would be a long time before he could erase the image from his mind, the image of this huge man, someone who looked like he took so much pride in his physique, obviously pumped weights, flopping in the driver's seat; head down, arms hanging by his sides.

And there was the smell to contend with. It had taken permanent residence in Jason's nostrils by now, had hung curtains, set up furniture even installed shag carpeting. He could almost taste it. He mentioned this to Sandra and she brought him an unopened Poland Spring from her car. He chugged half of it and swished it in his mouth.

Touching a corpse was disgusting, especially a muscular guy like the cop, all that muscle turned to jelly. The coldness was quite puke-inspiring as well. You hugged people all your life, poked them, high fived them, punched them, even had sex with them and you never wonder what they would be like cold and mushy.

He even knew the name of this process, *algor mortis,* when the heart first stops and the body gets cold, right before rigor mortis began. Jason remembered seeing a band advertised on a flyer called Al Gore Mortis.

Jason said a brief eulogy in the alley. Sandra kept trying to rush him, reminding him of the gravity of the situation. Jason complained that he felt guilty, treating dead bodies like trash, something that was a nuisance to be quickly discarded. It was still a human being. They should pay the proper respects.

"Do what you want," she said, walking back to her car. "Take your time, but hurry."

Who could argue with that logic?

***

When he got home, he asked Sandra to borrow her vacuum. She also gave him some carpet shampoo.

Before he turned away, she asked if he worked tomorrow. He told her he was off for two days.

"That's good. Maybe we can find those Serpentera babies. I'll call you. Answer your damn phone, please."

*Great. I was really hoping to get a day off from insanity.*

***

While scrubbing his apartment, he wondered about where the money came from.

A bright red gym bag full of cash. Whose cash? Did the cop rob a bank? Stick up a liquor store?

Jason counted the cash, sitting on his floor, stacking the bills up. Some of them were crudely bundled in masking tape. Eight thousand bucks, along with some cigarette butts, bottle caps, and a flyer from a strip club . . . random trash that accidentally got scooped up into the bag.

And the car. It was much too small for a big guy like that. Even Jason had to wrench the seat forward to get in. Of course, the other obvious thing: A marijuana leaf air freshener. The boys on the force probably wouldn't approve of that.

Jason cursed himself for not having a TV or internet service. He couldn't watch the news.

As soon as he woke up in the morning, at almost the crack of dawn, he went out trekking around the neighborhood to find an early edition of the newspaper. It wasn't easy. Being the crappy part of town, newspaper boxes were usually abandoned, just rusting graffiti-covered receptacles that housed God-knows-what these days.

He hiked quite far to no avail.

His back-up plan was to call Ms. Millman around nine o'clock and ask her if she knew something. She would. She had internet service. All he really had to do was sit tight until then. But he couldn't, not with that mysterious red gym bag sitting on his floor. He decided he might as well try to find a newspaper in the interim.

Ms. Millman didn't answer her phone right away. Nine o'clock turned into ten o'clock. Time was of the essence. He bought a bitter cup of coffee from a convenience store and sat in his apartment, waiting.

When she did answer, she had information in spades, albeit groggily.

The local news reported that a murderous attack, most likely gang related, occurred in the Northcrest Apartment buildings on the west side. The resident was a felon and a crack dealer named Terrance Holtz, who was found shot dead on the scene, a Glock 17 in his hand. Two others were shot dead, one was found with an axe imbedded in his shoulder. Another young man, Ronny Belton, was currently in critical condition at St. Gertrude hospital due to multiple lacerations believed to have been delivered by the same axe.

One of the perpetrators of the siege was Gary Denton, manager of a car dealership in Dunwoody, unmarried.

The sports car guy. Sandra said his picture was there and she recognized him. The web article provided very little else about him except that police were confused about his connection with the drug dealer.

The other perpetrator was William J. Scovis, five year officer in the local police force. His bullet ridden body was found miles away from the scene in a parked car. Of course, Jason knew this already. The article finally stated that police were undergoing an investigation of Scovis' mysterious departure from the scene.

"So," said Sandra, "it appears you have a huge bag of drug money sitting on your floor."

"That's everything in the article?"

"That's it, all nice and neat."

"Should I worry? I don't think so. It seems pretty clear that there's no connection to me, but then I worry because I feel a little over confident, you know, I see the brown blood splotches on my carpet then . . . "

"Jason, *relax*. Where did you go yesterday, before the cop came in?"

"I went to work, dealt with inconsiderate demanding jerks for about eight hours. A usual day. After that, I shared some suds with my homies."

"So, while these hideous characters were escaping from their respective morgues, you were humping it in the busiest bookstore in town. Then you were sucking down beers in, most likely, a crowded dive bar. That was about the time the gruesome twosome started cracking heads on the other side of town."

"I guess so."

"You couldn't ask for a better alibi. Don't worry. Find a nice safe place to stash the money in your apartment. That's all you have to do."

"It seems too easy."

"You got a gym bag full of cash. Stop whining. I wish I had your problems."

"I do need money."

"Just don't go spending it wildly around town. Don't put a down payment on a Benz or get gold plated teeth."

"Yeah, sure, I'm gonna haul ass to Lenox mall for some bling-bling."

"Stash it and forget about it, kiddo. Go about your normal routine, go to work, and keep buying generic stuff at Kroger. Don't think about the money."

"Shopping is the last thing on my mind. Trust me."

"Well, that's good. I need to go now. I have to grade some papers and jump in the shower. I have to teach a few classes this afternoon. It's a busy day for me."

"All right."

They hung up. A few minutes later, something else struck him, something important.

Carlos. The article didn't mention anything about Carlos, the last screamer.

*Maybe he's a special case*, he thought. He had died a day before all the other guys. Jason had seen his body lying face down in the grass right before Officer Scovis yelled at him and he was dragged away by Big Mama. Maybe his brain and body had atrophied too much in the course of that day to be reanimated by the squigglies. By witnessing Roger's return, it was apparent they didn't last too long. Maybe Carlos couldn't escape the morgue. Doing something like that couldn't be a walk in the park, even while possessed by a supernatural being.

A human body had limitations. At its essence, it was just meat and tissue, and those things didn't have a long shelf life. He was experienced in this. Dead bodies were squishy and useless, more apt to shrivel than get up and do the mambo.

Jason shoved the bag into his closet. He paused a second then reached in and took some bills. He shoved them into his wallet. The only times his wallet was this thick was when he was about to pay a bill with it, always just a temporary thickness.

He propped it up in the back of his closet and stacked two cardboard boxes on top of it, stuff that he had yet to organize.

*You can buy some furniture now, J-Man. You don't have*

*to wait months to become a manager. We can do it on the cheap, pick up some odds and ends, get this place looking suitable for human habitation.*

*You can score that octopus lamp this weekend.*

*Splurge, baby.*

Walking back into his den, three baby Serpenteras were cruising through the air, an orange-pink one, a purple one and a dark green one, fluttering in the air playfully, whooshing around him in greeting. He went into the laundry room to see about nine more, a few draped languidly across the washer, a few flying.

He remembered his joy at seeing the machine empty the day before. He rolled his eyes.

Laundry was becoming imminent. He had one pair of underwear left, two and a half pairs of socks, one t-shirt, and one pair of pants. He was sticking with the Mike Shibble rule for sure. No laundry in this room, ever.

He realized he was procrastinating, then started cleaning, especially the carpet that still had some dead cop residue. A few hours later, he swiped up his keys and headed down to Ross for some new clothes. Discount rack only. *That's fiscal discipline, baby!*

Next, Willie Chan's. His appetite wouldn't revive for a while but he knew he should try to eat.

His meal took forever. He saw the owner standing behind the counter, wearing a traditional Chinese suit, smiling at his ever increasing clientele. Julia's exquisite face arose in his mind which prompted him to phone Dave about Melanie's party. Dave didn't answer.

He floated a text message to Chris.

Chris was entering Jason's inner circle of friends at a rapid pace. It had been at least two years since he had a consistent pool of buddies to hang with.

*Even if it doesn't work out with Julia, I still got my pals.*

Sitting out in his car, the containers of food remained unopened. He was thinking about the dead disgusting cop.

The smell still lingered a bit. He removed a bottle of Texas Pete hot sauce he kept in his glovebox. *I'll nuke that taste out of my mouth if I have to!* He saturated his food with the hot sauce and forced himself to eat it.

Dave called. He was interested in the party. He mumbled something about another party going on, prefacing his description by saying it was far out in the sticks. He said Melanie's party sounded better, closer. It was within city limits, so if it bombed they could more easily escape. Not so with the party Dave mentioned. The long drive out to his friend's lake house committed them to be there until the wee hours.

"Well, there is one other reason I want to go to this party," Jason confessed. He told Dave about Melanie's roommate, and how there just *might* have been a spark there. He described their brief encounter.

"Damn right that was a spark!"

"Shut up. Don't jinx it. I don't like getting my hopes up with girls. The higher your hopes are the harder they fall."

Dave started making violin sounds.

"Real funny. We can't all be Mr. Suave McLadykiller like you."

"Sheesh. I wish. I've gotten lucky a few times this year. That's it. My powers are highly exaggerated."

"If you say so, stud muffin."

"Call me later when you hear from Chris. I have to go back to the sales floor and pretend to work."

Later at the diner, with a black coffee and a book, Chris rang him. He was on board. Jason was only half paying attention to him, watching his waiter doing a one-armed push-up in the middle of the floor. A waitress and a few cooks applauded him.

Walking out to his car, Jason thought he saw Carlos walk by, a guy staggering wearing a ball cap and a warm-up suit like his ex-roommate wore sometimes.

Nope. He was way off the mark. Carlos had worn a t-shirt

that night and couldn't have changed into new clothes as a bleeding-eared corpse.

# CHAPTER 7

TWO HOURS LATER, with Dave and Chris in his car he asked, "Are you guys noticing *extremely* strange behavior in people lately? Or is it just me?

He reminded them of Lotus and the bartender, the waiter at the diner, the springy thief from the day before, and the magician. They barely responded.

"How about that shooting on the west side of town?"

"What shooting?"

"A cop and some car salesman killed a drug dealer and ran out with a huge bag of money. It was on the news."

"Doesn't that happen every day?" said Chris.

Dave said, "Do you think the springy thief has something to do with it?"

The car exploded in laughter as it rolled out of the parking lot.

They cruised around a bit. Chris was thumbing through the CD holder. He chose one and stuck it in, some nineties grunge band he was embarrassed to own. He stopped to get some gas. After checking the time, Dave said it was too early to hit the party.

There was nothing more awkward than getting to a party too early. They played a shooting gallery video game outside of a gas station and got hit on by some staggering old hag, wearing a tube top and a short skirt, obviously hooking. She was younger than she looked, missing teeth, indicating a penchant for methamphetamines.

Carlos would probably have been a more welcomed sight. This chick was hideous. She sputtered on for a while, then announced she had a discounted "Back Door Special" for cute guys like them.

Chris gagged. Dave cracked up.

As she blathered on, Jason sized up the situation to decide if this was some variety of the new weirdness going around. Nope, he concluded it was just normal everyday vileness. Atlanta chocked full of it. It was part of its charm.

Dave wanted to pick up some food. Chris suggested they swing by Willie Chan's. Jason groaned.

"I had it for lunch. All week."

"I don't understand the popularity of that place. God knows what form of road kill is in that stuff. And all those multi-colored sauces . . . They just came out with a blue one!"

"No, it's more of a lime-green color."

"It's magenta!" said Jason sniggering.

They hopped into the car and decided on Taco Bell. This was Dave's choice.

"That is *so* much more upscale than Willie's." mocked Jason, as he drove.

They ordered from a drive through and ate in the parking lot.

***

The party was hitting its high point when they arrived, which is to say that the thirty to forty people in the ramshackle house were either loaded, drunk, stoned or just plain jazzed up on whatever mental deficiencies they brought along.

A table in the den was stacked with assorted bottles of booze and three different types of soda pop mixers. There were also a few plates of cookies, a mix of potato chips, a huge family pack of Funyuns, and fallen layers of a decimated birthday cake.

Melanie greeted them there. She introduced them to

whoever was paying attention. She said most of the guests were in the rec room watching Troma movies. *Bloodsucking Freaks* had just ended. Ever seen *The Toxic Avenger*?

They all nodded.

There was a trampoline in the back! One of their roommates, Josh had an Xbox with brand new disks, just purchased today. Did they like video games? Only Chris nodded.

In slurred speech, she also warned them that her ferret, Bilbo, had escaped from its cage and was at large.

"Don't sit on the couch. He sometimes nestles behind the cushions, in the den anyway. Just don't sit in the den until I find him, okey-dokey?"

They okey-dokied back. She led them into the movie room. As they walked along, Chris remarked, "I smell weed. I like weed."

About fifteen to twenty people were in there, sitting mostly on the floor, beers at their sides, some watching *The Toxic Avenger* and laughing, others chatting among themselves in clusters, most holding a bottle of beer, a red Solo cup or a wine glass. Some people had their own little pow-wow in the back, not watching the movie at all, gathered on a ratty couch under a huge Metropolis poster drooping from the wall.

The room was humid with bodies. It took him a while to scope out Julia. Two guys were on either side of her, enrapt in a spirited conversation. *Two fucking guys.* They looked like little cream-puff college jerks. The thick one looked kind of like a jock.

"That your girl right there?" asked Dave.

"Yep. Between those two morons."

"Don't get your panties in a bunch. You want to clunk her on the head and drag her back to your cave? Relax. Let's go grab some Funyuns."

Just then, their eyes locked. Her head dodged around bodies milling around her and her hand went up in an excited wave. She made a recoiling motion to the thick guy on her right then beamed a smile at Jason.

Jason shaped his hand around an invisible cup, and mouthed the word "Drink?"

She shook her head and pointed to a cup near her foot. She already had one.

He put up his palm and mouthed the words, "Right back".

In the den, sloshing rum and Dr. Pepper into Solo cups, David said, "She likes you, Romeo. That was no spark. That was a roaring bonfire!"

"Uh-huh. Man, she looks just like Jill."

"Forget your ex, dude. She's history."

"Yeah. Absolutely."

"Wylie, if you wus out on this I will rip off your eyelids with my teeth. You got that?"

"Yes, sir."

"If you let her slip away," said Chris. "I'm gonna find that ferret and beat you with it."

A toast, a tap of Solo cups, and they worked their way back to the screening of *The Toxic Avenger*. He had to give her credit, this was such an improvement to those freakily costumed space opera flicks Melanie usually presented. He thought maybe he had misjudged her tastes. The room was too crowded so they had to stand against the wall. They could barely see the big screen TV.

He couldn't see Julia. More people had stood up and were meandering around. Some more people squeezed into the door. He couldn't see those two guys either.

"This sucks," said Dave in reference to the incoming guests nudging and sliding in front of him. Excitement was building, the DVD movie losing noise supremacy, slowly being buried under the hubbub. They heard a scream and a shout from the back. Heads turned, backs formed a dome over some mysterious spot of interest.

Dave hastily shoved Jason into the den. Pretty soon, Melanie popped out of the room. Her drunken droopy gaze was funny.

"What's the commotion in there, Mel?"

"That Brett guy fell. Something happened to him. I don't know."

"Brett?"

"One of those guys talking to Julia. She wants to talk to you but hang on. She's helping Brett."

Melanie staggered away, saying, "Brett is stupid . . . "

"Sorry he's not dead, Jason," said Dave tapping him with his elbow.

"I don't want him dead. Why would I want him dead?"

It took a few seconds to break out of his serious mode.

*Did I cause that? Any squigglies around?*

Apparently they didn't give him the Carlos treatment, or the room would be freaking out.

Just gave him a little push. Or something.

Dave was too distracted to notice Jason's brief bout of paranoia. He was staring into his cup several seconds trying to determine if it was drinkable. The Dr. Pepper was quite flat. And warm. Chris seemed to enjoy it.

The house was filling up. This was the type of party they had both outgrown by about three years. Shit, maybe ten. That didn't make it a bad thing. Awkward, but not bad.

Dave didn't look too comfortable flattened against the wall. Jason felt extremely claustrophobic. A window was open down the hall. Sounds of mirth. People were out there. It was too nice of a night to spend inside a bit-too-humid house.

Jason nodded towards the back door. Melanie waddled by.

"Going outside," Jason muttered to her, not sure if she heard him.

In the back of his mind, he was knitting together a strategy. Outside would be a better place to chat with her, where he wouldn't have to exhaust himself shouting over the raucous din of partiers.

The ball was in fate's court now.

Chris peeked into the Xbox room, which also happened to be where the weed smell emanated.

"I'll check you dudes in a bit," he said with a wink.

He dove right in.

"He might never come out of there," remarked Dave, as he grabbed a handful of Ruffles. They refreshed their drinks and headed out the screen door to the back yard.

No one was jumping on the trampoline. Some kids were laying on it passing a joint. There was a volleyball game going on. A long-haired guy with a goatee explained the rules to them: whenever a team scored a point the other team had to drink. They also had to hit it one handed while holding onto their drinks. If they spilled or dripped any, they had to take a big sip.

Jason and Dave split off into different teams. Being the most sober, they got to serve and didn't have to hold their drinks while they played.

The other players were *really* polluted. They could barely stand up. This party was amateur central; most of the kids had probably freshly escaped from their parents' houses, into the arms of college life. They were still at the point where heavy drinking was an innocent novelty.

Ah, youth.

They were making him feel like an old man at twenty six.

While they were playing, Jason saw Julia come outside with Melanie. She towered over tiny roundish Melanie. That was the only real difference between her and Jill, height. Jill hadn't been abnormally short, 5 foot 6, but standing next to him, she did seem kind of midget-like. Jason was six foot one.

In fact he had considered that to be her only physical flaw. So Julia's height made her an even more perfect version of Jill.

Dave was right on cue. When it was his turn to serve, he aimed the ball directly at Julia who was obliviously leaning against the trampoline, chatting with Mel.

The contents in their cups went flying, soaking both girls. The trampoline stoners scattered. Dave shouted an apology, nodding for Jason to go smooth it over. Of course, Jason had already figured this out.

Neither girl was the least bit angry.

"My man Dave lacks proper depth perception, among other things."

Melanie had got the worst of it, holding out her soaked t-shirt from her breasts, giggling, shouting silly threats at Dave across the yard.

Julia explained that she didn't mind.

"I like being sticky," she said.

"I can get you a towel if you want, Jason said.

"That's okay, I'll just go change clothes real quick."

"Hurry back so you can help me whip Dave's ass in volleyball," he said.

"Challenge accepted. I'll be right back."

She sauntered away.

This game didn't last much longer. Julia joined up with Jason's team, after donning a thin hoodie over a green t-shirt. Melanie joined Dave's team, to keep things even. Dave let her serve a few and gave her some pointers. She could barely make it over the net. Her first serve hit a female teammate directly in the face, her drink exploding everywhere.

The game petered out from there. The players swayed, chatted and giggled to one another, then they just started wondering off or sitting down in the grass. Jason and Dave tried to keep it going but the game was officially killed off when someone stepped out onto the back deck and shouted, "We found Bilbo!"

Mel went running up to the house, hands flapping, giggling. Jason and Julia talked about sports. Jason asked her if she ever played sports. Not much besides lawn darts, some bowling, some skating. Jason was praising his only athletic interests: air hockey, skee-ball, and fooz ball.

Inside Melanie cradled little Bilbo and invited everyone to pet him as the little critter squirmed in her arms. Chris stood with them eating a huge hunk of chocolate cake, his red eyes locked on the ferret. They milled around a little more until Dave suggested they all hit a diner or a Waffle House, some extra birthday festivities for Julia.

Dave described his craving for "a late night omelet with some kind of ungodly shit stuffed into it".

The party was winding down anyway. The other two roommates were staying until the rest of the stragglers went home or passed out. The girls went and got their coats.

Jason didn't see Brett. He had long forgotten him.

They all crammed into Jason's car, his crew and the two girls. Another car was going to follow them. They went to Billy's in Buckhead, a slightly more upscale and expensive diner than a regular greasy spoon joint.

Julia didn't hesitate to sit directly beside Jason at the table. That was a good sign. If she had scurried to the other side where most of the girls were sitting, some momentum could have been lost.

Their interests were very similar. Julia wasn't quite the overt bookworm that Jill had been, maybe more into the visual arts. She liked some of the same underground-type comics that he liked, especially Robert Crumb, Harvey Kurtzman, and Art Spiegelman.

She said she was dying to indulge more into literature of all stripes, but was too busy with school.

"Real reading is a luxury I don't have these days," she explained.

"With me, it's a sickness!" said Jason.

He gushed on about a lot of crime writers he had been into for the last few years. He suggested a few, saying someone didn't need too much spare time to read them; they were such fast fun reads. He described some Jim Thompson books he had read. She sounded interested.

"Don't waste your money buying them. Hey, I'm the hook-up there. I'll loan them to you."

"Oh, that sounds great. Send them my way."

The waiter brought over the birthday omelet jutting a huge candle. The book discussion made Chris bring up the subject of Jason's possible promotion. Of course, Chris tweaked the truth a bit to mean, "Jason's getting promoted!"

Cheers all around, chucks on the shoulders, beers raised in celebration. Jason tried to explain that it wasn't certain by any means but everyone was too drunk and rowdy to absorb these little details. At the three o'clock position of the large round table, he noticed Dave between two other girls from the party, blabbing away about something. Chris was still bleary-eyed and spaced out, talking with some scruffy stoner from the party.

Jason and Julia discussed movies for about an hour until Melanie suggested karaoke. They all drove to a late night karaoke place. Everyone Jason knew stayed all the way to the end. One of the girls and the stoner guy stayed around almost to the end. That guy was a serious talker. He and Chris shared an interest in video games.

Eventually, Dave and Chris fell asleep on the red sectional sofa in the singing booth.

Jason forced himself to stay awake and entertain the ladies. He couldn't believe how much energy those girls had. It was bottomless.

He and Julia danced a little, held hands, some vaguely sexual touchy-touchy, their bond gelling at warp speed.

It was funny how that works. For months, it seemed he was invisible to women. Since Jill, he had been on two or three dates with nice girls, but nothing transpired. Even though they were girls he thought he had something in common with.

Nothing happened for a long time, then . . .

*This.*

He had gotten her phone number when they were at Billy's. By the time they stumbled out of the karaoke place, the sky had turned a dim gray color, dawn just peeking through. Everyone was asleep, except for them on the ride home. Chris was snoring, mumbling something in his sleep that kept them entertained.

Outside of the girls' house, he squeezed her hand and said he'd call her later to check up with her.

"You did well, young Jedi," said Dave on the way back, barely awake, his head leaning against the passenger's side window.

***

He crashed on Dave's couch and slept until two o'clock that afternoon. He called Julia about six that evening. Since neither he nor she had plans that night, he offered to take her out for dinner.

Or just hang out. Do whatever. She said sure. She even sounded happy about it.

During their conversation, he slipped in a question about the incident with Brett. He was pretty sure a Serpentera had been involved, but not one hundred percent. He had been too transfixed on Julia to give it much attention.

"Oh, he hurt himself baaad," she said with a pointedly mocking tone. "He might even be in *critical* condition."

Strangely, she started laughing very hard.

He ended the conversation saying he'd pick her up later.

# CHAPTER 8

HE WENT TO his house to shower and change clothes. He also needed to refresh his wallet with the gym bag loot.

There was a yellow Post-it note on his door. Scribbled on it was a simple message, *call me*. It was signed by Sandra and was underlined.

He decided to wait until he was cleaned up and changed before he called her. In fact, he decided he would call her on the way to Julia's house. He didn't want to risk her barging over to his apartment, slowing him up, derailing his mind with Serpentera drama.

*Give a guy a break!* Couldn't he get a few days for himself and do something pleasant for a change?

Apparently not.

In the car, with one hand on the steering wheel, he dialed her up.

"Good Lord, it's about time!" she said when she answered. "I thought maybe you were avoiding me."

"Oh, I was just engaging in this thing called a *life*. You know, where I have friends and stuff. I even met a girl."

"Oh, wonderful."

This remark was saturated in sarcasm.

"Oh, gee, thanks for the lukewarm urine shot to my enthusiasm. You know, I've only been ignored by every single woman in this town since my ex dumped me a year ago. I don't expect you to care anyway."

"Sorry. I need you. It's just awful timing. We have to find those babies. I need your concentration on this. This is a really delicate time. Are you sure you can't cancel your date?"

"Are you serious?"

"Well, can you?"

"Shit, no. I'm on my way there *now*!"

"We need to go down into the lair. There's this psychic thing I can do that may help us locate them, but I need your participation as soon as possible."

"Tomorrow. Maybe. A big maybe."

"Damn it! Please, don't do this."

"No fucking way!"

"Don't bring the girl over to your house."

"I'm not that stupid. It'll kill the mood having my little squiggly slug critters roaming around. I don't have the gigolo skills to hook that up anyway."

"We really need to talk. I mean, *really* need to talk."

"We're talking!"

"Don't bring her to your house. I've never seen a Serpentera in a state like she's in. Call me first thing tomorrow."

"Okay."

He parked in front of the house. He tipped some of the bottled water he had been drinking into his hand and swept it through his hair. His longish curly hair always needed a bit of taming.

Julia looked even better. She was wearing a long powder blue coat with a yellow fur collar. Her short blond hair was teased out to the sides. Art major girls always had best sense of style.

From the kitchen, she brought out two blue canvas bags that looked stuffed with something.

"Do you like kimbab? I made some."

"Sure."

"My brother gave me a kimbab-making kit for my birthday. I just tried it out today. They're kind of funky looking, but don't be afraid. I made some sandwiches, too, in case they frighten you."

"I'll eat anything that doesn't move."

"My sandwiches don't move."

"Nice. What kind are they?"

"Remember Bilbo?"

He laughed. From the bathroom, Melanie shouted, "I heard that!"

He had a list of things in his head that they could do. He and Dave had brainstormed this at his house.

There were two or three small bars that had bands playing. There were a few art galleries sprinkled here and there, one of the artists he was even vaguely familiar with. Little Five Points usually had something interesting happening on Saturdays. He was mainly going to wing it, but if inspiration didn't properly show itself, he needed a back-up plan.

There was no use in trying to pretend to be some super suave man-about-town. He couldn't pull that off anyway. He could be funny, even charming in his best moments. But he couldn't plan. Plans were for dullards and control freaks anyway. Everything considered, he could afford that one flaw.

They decided to get things rolling by walking around midtown. He thought to start out here because it was close to the High Museum. She was into art. That was a no-brainer. There was a street festival down there, too. That was an added bonus. Shit to look at to avoid awkwardness.

There was still an hour's worth of daylight hanging around so they could take in the sights. There was a lot of folk art, jewelry, and some paintings. When they walked by Beecher's Coffee on Peachtree Street, Julia suddenly turned at the window and waved. Inside, a short barista girl waved back at her.

"I used to work with this chick," she explained, then dove inside to chat with her, waving excitedly. The girl was very chipper back, in her green smock and little round glasses. She gave them free coffee. She apologized that she couldn't sneak them a scone.

"You're putting yourself in enough jeopardy sneaking the coffee," said Julia. "A scone would mean prison for damn sure!"

Gigglefest.

It was here he learned that she worked part-time at the Beecher's Coffee branch near Georgia State University. He found it weird that he knew so much about her personality, but didn't know where she worked. Maybe that was a good sign. Punch-a-time-clock jobs were ultimately interchangeable and revealed very little about one's inner core. This showed that they were interested in deeper aspects of each other.

Walking through mid-town, just as their conversation lulled and boredom seemed to be rearing its head, his eyes fell upon a hobby store window full of toy remote control airplanes stacked high. He hadn't played with these things since he was a teenager. He had a remote controlled helicopter as a ten-year-old boy and played with it until it fell apart.

He remembered seeing some kids flying these things in the park one day and being slightly envious.

Now, he had money to throw around on frivolous things. He'd almost forgotten about his loaded gym bag. Playing with these RC toys would be more fun than watching an eight dollar Hollywood stinker in some mall.

He swept his arm under hers and pulled her inside. His eyes hungrily roamed over the glass cases. At first she thought it was silly and suggested they go to Toys R Us for real toys for him.

"I guess they are kind of cute," she finally admitted.

"Don't say that about a Man toy."

"Man toy . . . "

He told her to pick one out. He'd buy it.

"You'll love it. Didn't you ever dream of being a pilot?"

"You're clearly hyping now. Don't hype."

"It's like flying . . . vicariously."

"It's like flying but you're actually playing with a toy."

"Pretty much."

"I'm sold."

She whipped around so joyously it was obvious she wasn't so sophisticated she wouldn't like flying a toy airplane.

"I'm gonna get the most badass plane here."

"Just don't get the A-10 Warthog. I got dibs on that sucker."

She told him not to waste his money. He told her to shut up and pick! She chose the red Biplane.

This was another good sign. He'd been worried she might be a little snooty. Sometimes high GPA college girls were a bit stuck up. For good reason, quality deserved quality after all. She had earned her scholarship through her own efforts, intelligence emanated from her. She probably was on the honor roll all through high school. It wasn't like she was some rich kid or sorority stuck-up, just smart. A sorority snoot queen wouldn't fly RC toys with a badly groomed retail employee.

Jason wasn't such a picky shopper. Within five minutes, he decided which style of Warthog he wanted. The clerk stood ready.

Their eyes widened a little when he pulled out the cash. He forgot about the huge wad he had stuffed into his wallet. He quickly scanned the bills to make sure there were no blood stains.

"You deal drugs, J-Money?"

*If you only knew where this money came from.*

"I got a big tax return last year," he explained.

They walked down to Piedmont Park, after stopping by the car to get the bags of food.

On the way to the park, he asked one more time about Brett, about how badly he had hurt himself.

"Why do you care about him? Did you know that guy?"

"Not a bit. Just curious."

"Well, he didn't get hurt at all. He just tripped over a bean bag chair. Melanie was playing around and pushed him. She likes him a little bit. God knows why. He's retarded. Don't tell her I told you, okay?"

"No problemo."

No Serpenteras were involved.

*It was all in my mind, my sick, twisted little jealous mind.*

It was a little crowded, lots of dog-walkers, skaters; the annoying type of people that always took up a lot of space. They scouted around a while to find a decent open spot without people laying around, throwing Frisbees or too much tree coverage.

The sun hovered bright orange, sinking just below the tree line. Daylight was going fast.

He was surprised at how technically adroit she was at assembling and navigating the toy airplane. She was almost better than he was. Some people were hopeless with these things. He did manage to get his up and flying freely, while hers hovered low, just circling.

Jason was curious to find out how far he could fly it. It struggled upward, the little plastic remote buzzing in his hand, then suddenly it jetted forward, like a real A-10 Warthog might have done during Battle of the Bulge. It disappeared from his sight, then returned coming forward at him, full speed.

Jason hit the ground. The plastic propeller nicked his ear.

Julia was squealing in laughter.

He spun around trying to find it. Julia pointed up. It was hovering there, battle ready. Jason noticed a thin purplish-pink light spiraling around its fuselage.

Uh-oh.

A baby Serpentera. It was playing with him.

Why now of all times? He would have a talk with Ms.

Millman. He would ask her to use her Serpentera language to inform them to stay out of his personal life. He had to draw a line in the sand.

"My little plane is acting funny, too," said Julia.

It was doing figure eights in the air. She held out the control box for him to see.

"I'm not even using the controls!"

Of course, a purplish-pink color flashed off of it as it zoomed around in the air.

"I guess they're defective!" He said with a forced grin.

Secretly he was worried. This wasn't a good time for these critters to get cheeky.

Close by, a little dog started yapping. Then another little dog joined it. Jason couldn't see too well, but knew they were yapping at the strange creatures that were flying above them.

As he took his eyes of the Warthog, it dived in to attack. Julia jumped out of the way just in time and flattened out on the grass. The biplane spun crazily in small circles, its back tailfin sticking out like a weathervane.

Julia was still laughing, sat up. As she was bending over the Warthog zoomed in for the kill. The biplane surged forward towards Jason, like a buzzing deranged, dive-bombing hornet. He swiped at it and the plane deftly avoided his fist quick as a hornet, too. Jason ran to Julia and grabbed the shoulders of her coat.

"Let's run!"

He grabbed the bags of food as a pink Frisbee connected with the back of his head.

Julia started laughing harder. She got whacked by a squeaky dog toy, and shouted, "Eeewwww, slobber!"

An apple core bounced off him, then a flip-flop whacked his head.

"We're under attack! Good God. The whole park is against us!"

"I think it's Al Qaeda!" he said.

As they ran, they could hear the buzzing of the RC planes right on their backs.

Jason spotted a large stone archway, just big enough for them to fit inside. There were some spider webs and a little trash, but it was otherwise safe.

They heard one of the planes crash on the outside. They watched as the little red biplane kamikazied into a large oak tree, plastic scattering in all directions. No better time for a make-out session.

Julia said drowsily, "I really wanted to take that red plane home. I'm kind of sad."

"That biplane was possessed by Satan. I'm glad you didn't!"

"I'll get you another one if you're that bad off. China cranks out ten every hour."

"That's okay."

He put his arm around her, smiling, shaking his head. Clever little buggers, those Serpenteras. They were always helping him. They knew exactly what to do, what he needed. Somehow they knew tossing in a little danger would torque up the romance. They were like his little guardian angels, if not better.

Some noisy kids were walking over the bridge, over their heads. Their stern mother spat rebukes. A half-chewed wiener on a stick dropped down in front of them.

"Nasty."

"Now, that's pleasant," she told him. "So many uncouth people out there. Ever get tired of so many inconsiderate people?"

"More than you know. That's all I see at my job every day."

He described a few of his notoriously bad customers, rude, pushy demanding people.

"Customers treat me the same way. God forbid you should skimp on one drop of soy milk in their precious little drinks."

"The public doesn't allow mistakes. Because they are customers, anyone with a name tag must drop at their feet when they walk in, robotically programmed to satisfy their whims."

"Yep."

He suggested another place near where he lived. It had a lake and, most importantly, no crowds.

"A trip to Decatur sounds good. We'll have our picnic out there!"

Another brief kiss. They started to gather their things when a curious sound erupted above them; something had struck the tree again. This wasn't made of hard plastic though. It was more of a wet sound. A few dribbles of gore rained down, then the entire dog carcass dropped into the grass near them.

Julia shrieked and covered her face. "Somebody threw a dog at the—"

"Don't look at it. Let's get going. Fast."

Nothing else weird happened on their way back to the car.

*Kids, you got a really sick sense of humor. You murdered an innocent little dog.*

Ms. Millman was definitely going to hear about this.

***

He knew of the perfect spot for their picnic. Once upon a time the place belonged to Mr. McCullen. Jason never knew much about him. The old geezer had been friends with his dad when they had rented a house close by. Jason had been given carte blanche to roam around on it as much as he wanted. At some point in his pre-teen years, Mr. McCullen had built a small lake into the ground and stocked it with fish. Jason used to drink beers here as a teenager. He smoked his first doobie in this place, not a habit that ever grew on him.

He had even done some fishing here, during the brief time he was into fishing.

He had always wanted to bring a girl to this spot but it was so secluded, he'd been afraid they would be creeped out. It had a slasher-movie look to it with all of its dead leaning trees. The quietness and the strange stillness was uncommon with the rest of town.

Julia seemed like the type of girl that didn't have that

kind of distrust. She probably could even handle herself against a machete wielding psycho. She came off like that.

As he parked, he realized it looked even worse. Trash floated on the still, muddy looking water, with some cans sticking out, too. There was some kind of indiscernible film on the top of the water like someone had discarded motor oil into it. People were such slobs. Assorted trash lay strewn about the dirt clearing. The stench of a dead animal permeated the air: a deer probably.

"Sorry, this place has gone so downhill. I seem to remember it being a lot nicer."

"This is nice. I like it."

She sounded sincere.

Jason shut off the engine.

He showed her around: the old oak tree he used to climb up, the old shed he and his buddies would use as their private drinking lodge, the old stump he used to shoot bottles off of with his BB gun. His dad had bought Jason the gun thinking he could "make a man" out of him, a varmint-shootin' hunter like himself.

Yeah, right. Shooting bottles and cans was fun though.

There was an old picnic table there, but it looked water-logged with fuzzy patches of mold. Julia had folded up a cloth inside one of the bags. She spread it out on the hood of the car and they had their picnic there. Jason uncapped a bottle of convenience store wine he picked up and poured them two paper cups full.

Julia put her hand up.

"Wait. Let's eat first."

He mentally cursed his alcoholic tendencies. When he saw booze, he had to drink it, right away.

As they ate, she told him more about herself. She had been hoping to get to NYU, but was doing Georgia State University for now. She had applied for a program overseas, in Paris. She was keeping her fingers crossed.

Jason chimed in by saying he knew an art history teacher

at Georgia Perimeter College, named Sandra Millman. Julia said she hadn't heard of her. He described some of her work. He started describing one painting in particular, then he realized he was describing Serpenteras. They were, after all, quite an inspiration to her.

"That sounds really interesting," she said, chewing Kimbab.

Another make-out session erupted after they finished their meals.

"We're kind of attracted to each other, you think?" she said, with a little smile.

"Yep," he said, and raised his little cup.

"To you, master aviator," he said.

She raised hers, too, "To you, my newly discovered toy plane enthusiast!"

They sipped and fell silent. Another round of making-out ignited, heavier this time with her sliding underneath him on the slippery cloth. He was propped up on his arm in a very uncomfortable position, but was afraid to move too drastically in order to not destroy the moment.

At last she laughed.

"It's a bit awkward up here, but nice."

"I agree but if you want . . . "

A heavy blunt thud sounded in his ears, echoing in his skull. Light flashed behind his eyes as Julia's forehead collided with his. Hard. Pain erupted, like a piece of metal turning in his skull. Julia wheezed a painful cry, her face falling forward. This was a moment he would replay in his mind forever.

That last soulful dark sigh of consciousness.

Everything else rolled out in agonizing slow motion.

He saw the back of her pretty blond head was trickling blood. As he looked up and his eyes refocused, he saw the slack face of his ex-roommate, Carlos, his grayish mouth hanging open, his arms extended over his head, both hands gripping something.

*Carlos*. Jason could barely recognize him. In the back of his mind, he had been expecting him.

Expecting him in some form. But a deadly, weapon-wielding Carlos was unexpected.

Jason anticipated his next move, stood up and lunged at him.

The Carlos creature flailed backwards, but Jason still managed to bring him down. Jason's knee struck a sharp rock, incapacitating it for several seconds, long enough for it to retrieve his weapon. He caught Jason on the shoulder as Jason attempted to stand up.

Luckily, creature wasn't too fast. As it went down, Jason hoisted a large rock. Cold, mushy hands grappled out at him. Jason snatched off one of the living dead man's fingers. It fell out of his hand as he reached out blindly, dug his hand into Carlos' bicep, and slung the rock at the dead man's face. It tumbled backwards, but Jason did too as he tripped over one of the long strips of deadwood on the ground.

He didn't know exactly when he noticed part of Big Mama dangling out of its ear.

He thought: *Hurry up! Help me.*

After hitting it with the rock, the Carlos monster lost power quickly, swaying on its feet, stumbling backwards. Jason saw Big Mama dangling out of its ears, both sides. She lit up and it straightened, regaining some strength.

Seeing her like this took Jason off his guard. He assumed Big Mama was going to save him. He lost several crucial seconds. He felt around for a solid weapon and found a small petrified log, a thick one. He lunged forward with it, jousting style, towards the thing's stomach.

It fell back into the lake with a loud splash. Big Mama and a smaller pinkish spindle hovered over the water like tiny flying eels. They were vibrating. He knew enough about them to know that vibrating Serpenteras meant crazy Serpenteras.

Or angry Serpenteras. Whatever. It wasn't good.

Then he realized *why* they were angry.

They were angry because they didn't succeed in killing him.

*Big Mama just tried to kill me.*

The little ones at Piedmont Park weren't being playful. They were trying to send a message from the mafia don of Serpenteras.

A psychotic Serpentera is very, very bad.

He watched them hover there as if expecting a verbal explanation.

"What the hell's wrong with you?" He said as he felt around his pants for his cell phone. It was in the car.

He dove into the front seat for his cell phone and dialed 911.

An eternity passed waiting for the ambulance to get there. Directions were hard to explain.  Driving here was second nature to Jason, but describing it wasn't so easy. The pitch blackness was an issue as well.

He ran all the way out to the main road, almost a mile, to make sure the ambulance would find it.

Julia was unconscious. She wasn't dead, but suffered a severe blow, which she probably wouldn't wake up from for a long time. He got just the information about her riding in an ambulance. Even that wasn't a lot. They mainly sought information from him: What was she hit with? How hard do you think the attacker struck her?

Julia looked dead. She wasn't, but she surely looked that way. They carefully wrapped her head and moved her around as little as possible. He kept asking them, "She's not dead, right?"

The EMTs just looked at him sympathetically, never outright saying, "She's in a coma."

A coma was as close to dead as you could get.

Of course, the police confronted him at the hospital. He told them everything. He rode back to the spot with them and showed them the weapon the Carlos creature had used on her. And he showed them Carlos, still on his back, his toes sticking up in the murky water.

"Did you know this guy?" asked one of the cops.

"Believe it or not," he answered, "I did."

***

At the police precinct, it got more interesting. They questioned him but not in the way presented in TV cop shows. He spent most of his time in a chair at the sergeant's desk, just listening to them prattle. They offered him some cookies. Nothing very intimidating. Just all the basic questions.

The only real memorable moment was when a cop sat down with a folder and tried to figure out all the bizarre facts.

"So this attacker . . . " he started, trying to find the exact words, "was your ex-roommate, right?"

"Um-hmmm."

"Carlos Fredrico Vasquez. He was presumed dead last week."

"I heard something about that, yes."

"In case you don't know this, which I'm sure you don't, he was presumed dead after driving a car into someone's house. The people in the house were on some kind of hallucinogens, screaming about huge slugs crawling across the walls. One of the people started firing a gun wildly through the house. Did you hear about that? The news did a little story on it."

"No, I didn't."

What a lie.

"One of our officers choked to death on something while patrolling the road. It's weird."

Sarge paused.

"Forget it. I won't get into that. It doesn't matter."

He slapped his hands on his desk. He reopened the folder.

"Getting back to *Senior* Vasquez . . . He wasn't dead. It appears that he suffocated on something. What it was? Who knows? All of his vital signs had dropped to zero, confirmed by the guys in the ambulance that picked him up from the house. He was dead. Dead as . . . well, just dead. As they were taking him to the hospital downtown, he just got up out of the gurney, unzipped himself and started walking away."

"But he was supposed to be dead?"

"Apparently. I guess they got it wrong. They tried to stop him and he started running. He ran directly into four lanes of traffic."

"Weird."

"Uh-huh. One or two people said they saw him walking around your neighborhood, kind of lumbering around like a zonked out freak. The fella had some kind of messed up skin disease. His face looked like it was peeling off."

"Yuck."

"I guess he hid out there at the lake, huh?"

"Creepy."

"That was private property, by the way. You had no business there, son."

"Sorry."

The old cop looked like he wanted to lecture, but was too tired.

"The owners aren't upset. They remembered you."

"My dad probably knows them. They are the McCullen's. I don't remember their first names. We've known them from way back."

"They spotted Carlos running there today, lurking around the woods. The coincidence is strange."

No kidding.

"It's just so bizarre," the cop said. "Lots of really strange things have been happening around here, Twilight Zone material for sure."

Jason nodded.

***

Jason called Melanie. She and the other roommates were at the hospital. He had to review the same horrible story once again. She was broken up of course. Julia's situation hadn't improved. There was no way to tell if or when she would ever improve. Not good.

He told her over and over he was sorry.

*"I knew the guy. He was my ex-roommate. He went insane, wandering out in the woods, all deranged. I should have done more. There had to be some way I could have stopped him."*

Melanie could never comprehend the sick truth here.

She didn't understand how he could feel responsible. After all, he had beaten the attacker away. They went round and round like this. Melanie was sensitive and apologetic to the point of annoyance. He got a taste of this with the Roger incident.

She mentioned that.

"There are so many bad things going around these days . . . "

More apologies and baby talk, boo hoo, boo hoo, how sad, what a cruel world, blah, blah, blah. At this point, he wanted to hit something, not cry; an incident like this required fierce retaliation not navel gazing tears, fake maudlin crap. Even if the culprit was Fate herself, she had to be held accountable, the cold hearted bitch.

*Rage, Melanie. Give it a try! It doesn't hurt to get your hackles up once in a while!*

Julia was a young girl with so much potential, such a great life ahead of her. Intelligence, beauty, a great understanding of the world; all this talent and it didn't seem to go to her head. She was down to earth, grounded, a mixture of high and low; a trait so rare in people. She could have lived a life of inspiration for the world.

She;s the one that gets a coma? Good God, what a world.

Hadn't the cruel wheel of fate ruined enough innocent people up to now? When was enough, enough?

The girl of his dreams might be gone, just like that. He got merely a sneak-peek at happiness before it was savagely pulled away. Right then, he didn't want to get into the more selfish aspects of his pain.

There would be plenty of time for that later.

Melanie warned him to stay away from the hospital because her parents were there, upset and angry with him. Her tone suggested they were more than just angry.

"I'll bet they are."

"They suspect you guys were doing something dirty up there. I'll keep you posted on her condition. Please don't show up over here, 'kay?"

"I got it. Thanks, Mel."

Next was Dave on the line. He was just calling to get the details about the date. Jason spilled the news in sparse details, explaining that he couldn't go over it again.

"Don't make me relive this shit again. Please."

"I totally understand."

Dave said he was sorry over and over. He invited him to crash over at his place. Jason had planned to ask him anyway.

Going back home was out of the question, at least not until he spoke to Sandra.

Dave was one hell of a guy, and one hell of a friend. Dave cancelled a night out with an old friend to stay with Jason, to try to cheer him up. Not that it was possible. They considered going around the block to shoot some pool at a bar, something tame and quiet, if he felt up to it later. Jason knew it was too soon for that.

Jason stepped out on the back porch with a beer and his phone. He took several long pulls from the bottle before he gathered up the nerve to dial Sandra's number.

Even she was shocked by what he told her. He laid out everything in vivid detail, being careful not to miss a note. He wanted her to get a good understanding of what transpired.

"Oh, my God. I'm so sorry, Jason."

"That doesn't help much, but thanks."

"Damn. I told you Big Mama was on edge but even I didn't expect her to strike so soon. Of course, she did it because she's—"

Sandra stopped very abruptly.

"Because she's what?"

"What do you think?"

"I'm asking *you*."

"Please. I'm begging you. Stop talking like that."

"I'm not talking like anything."

"Yes, you are. You're talking in passive-aggressive code shit. Spill it. Big Mama is what?" Jason said.

"She's *jealous*, you big idiot! Why is it so hard for you to understand?

"Jealous. What do I have to be jealous of?"

"You. She's crazily in love with you, has been from the start."

He didn't really know what to say.

"I know it's weird to think about . . . "

"Well, yeah!"

"I know you will never have the same feelings for her and I don't expect you to. She probably realizes this, too, down deep. It's just lately with her kids missing then you two-timing her . . . "

"*Two-timing*?"

"I'm just saying try to be more understanding of her feelings right now."

He couldn't believe he hadn't figured this out. It had been so obvious, yet, with all the strange things going on so rapid-fire, he missed the signs. He confessed this to Sandra.

"Well, that's completely understandable. I don't mean to push you so hard."

"About the missing Serpenteras," he began. "Isn't it possible they could have died after lodging themselves in those peoples' throats? Thought about that yet? Some of them were probably killed at that house. Someone was shooting a gun."

Sandra started to speak up. He talked over her.

"You just have to you use your Serpentera language skill to explain that to her. I'll try to smooth things over from my end, however possible."

"Twenty of them are missing. Sure, three or four could have died in those bodies but there are about fifteen unaccounted for. Big Mama can't scope them out telepathically like she should be able to. They aren't responding to her homing signals. They could have traveled far out of range, or gotten weak from lack of energy, which could kill them fast. Either way, they are probably dead. We need to find out what killed them. Whatever did it could get Big Mama too."

"Please excuse me, though, if I'm not brimming with sympathy for her. She destroyed a poor girl's life tonight."

"So that's *it*? It's terrible what happened but please don't give up yet."

"That is easier said than done."

"You can't. It's too late to back out."

"Look, I didn't ask for this. My normal life burns me out enough. I didn't ask to be part of your Serpentera cult and I need to get out."

"That's too bad. You're in it, buddy."

"All I did was sign an apartment lease, for God's sake. Under extenuating circumstances, too!"

"It's more, let's say, *involved* than that, Jason."

She sighed into the phone.

"I wanted to wait until the right time to tell you this. I was hoping to explain this face to face because it's pretty shocking."

"Go ahead. Shock me."

She paused and sighed. She backed off, said they'd discuss it later.

"Nope. Too late. Do it."

"All right. So. Jason, do you know what a *succubus* is?"

He thought hard about this before answering. "That's something from mythology, right? A Greek or Roman mythological something-or-other?"

"It's in the Cabala, actually. It's not mythological because Big Mama is one, has the ability of one anyway."

"Okay . . . "

"Do you know what they do?"

"I think so."

"Think deeply. The days, before you saw the baby Serpenteras in your washing machine, do you remember having some vivid sexual dreams?"

"I'm a guy, Sandra, of course I have those. And, yeah, I had a memorable one around that time."

The reality slammed him.

He wanted to laugh it was so ridiculous. But it wasn't ridiculous. It made perfect sense. "Oh, my God. So . . . "

"So?"

"So, like, she *raped* me in my sleep?"

"That's such a harsh way to put it."

"Not to me!"

"You're entitled to feel however you want to feel about it. Don't shoot the messenger here, okay? I didn't put her up to it. I'm just as shocked as you are. I never knew they were capable of breeding with humans. I thought they would use some other conduit, bugs, snakes or even slugs, but she chose *you.*"

He couldn't respond. He thought about just hanging up.

*Please no more of this.* Can't process it. Overload. Danger, Will Robinson! Doesn't compute. Doesn't compute. La, la la, I can't hear you anymore . . .

"Jason, are you still there? C'mon."

"I'm here, unfortunately. I don't think I believe you. Maybe you got your facts mixed up."

"Oh, no. Uh-uh. Good God, kid. You think she would have done all these things for you because you dumped rotting leftovers in a washing machine? Serpenteras are highly advanced, intelligent creatures. You've been a witness to that. You think she's some kind of house pet, you bastard?"

"Hey, calm down."

"No, you need to hear this. Don't you realize everything she's done for you? She risked her children, all of her physical energy, and believe me, it's almost deadly for them to possess human beings like they do. Of course, their methods aren't particularly ethical from our standards . . . "

"Yeah, killing people isn't too impressive."

"Well, they are just babies. They didn't do anything any other animal in the wild wouldn't do to protect their habitat, to protect *you*. The older Serpenteras actually have quite a humane sense of right and wrong about them."

"They really expressed that today! Hoo boy!"

"Most of the time."

"Yeah. I got it. Big Mama is all worked up, turning into a psycho and don't patronize me because, damn it, you old hag, I've got a life too and I just can't process this no matter how hard you try. Just leave me alone for now because I've had an awful day and probably the weirdest one at that. Got it? Can I finish my beer, please?"

"Sure. I'll go down to the lair and see if I can patch things up. Where are you, by the way?"

"I'm at a friend's house. I'm staying here tonight."

"Good. Do that. I'm going down to the lair now and check things out."

"Be careful."

"I'm not worried. Call me tomorrow morning before you go home. Make sure it's, um, safe for you to go home. I'm pretty sure it is but . . . "

"I'm going home tomorrow. If she still wanted to kill me, she would have done it already. I'm still here, on my buddy's back porch, alive and well and trying to process everything."

"That's good."

"*Trying*."

"Okay. I'll talk to you tomorrow."

They hung up. He just sat there, drinking his beer. Static filled his mind. A little while later, Dave came outside and asked him how he was doing.

Dave assumed the phone conversation had something to do with Julia.

Jason just shrugged.

"You look white as a ghost, J-man. Hang in there, bro."

"I'm just sick. I feel like I'm in a suspended state of barfing. I'll probably be like this for a while."

# CHAPTER 9

HE TOOK A personal day from work the next day. He explained the situation to Janet.

"Aw, honey, that's too bad. You've been going through some really bad stuff lately. It's pretty slow here. Don't worry. Rest up."

"Thanks."

He and Dave sat around in the morning, watching TV and drinking black coffee. Jason discovered a *Smokey and the Bandit* DVD set on Dave's shelf and they watched that all morning.

Snappy dialog and car chases were medicine for the brain.

On the way home, he stopped by Willie Chan's for some lunch. The place was packed with a line going out the door. He noted to himself its rise in popularity over the last year. Previous times, it was sparsely filled with shabbily dress people folks like him, people who scraped up pocket change for such a meal. The staff usually appeared bored and laconic.

Lately, it was much more on the uptick. The place was a simmering ball of energy now.

He felt justified going here now. He could rub it into the faces of the Willie Chan's naysayers, the people who made fun of him for eating there so often.

*See, Dave? The food can't be too shitty with this kind of public support.*

But the long slow lines these days were a bit annoying. Last time he had waited a while too.

A poster on the window announced a new store opening on the other side of town; a new store to go with their new spicy sauce.

*Go Willie Chan's! Moving on up.*

As he drove up his street, he was annoyed to see someone parked in his usual spot along the curb. Even worse, there was a guy standing outside of his car, propped up against it, arms folded over his chest, looking around. He looked like he was lost.

*Stupid bozo.*

Jason had to go down the road, turn around and then park behind him. His car could barely fit between it and the driveway next door. The house was basically abandoned, but he still didn't like the back of his car poking out over a driveway. That meant he would have to come back out and move it later.

He shut the engine off and tried not to look at the guy, knowing he would have something snarky to say to him. He didn't like to be snarky. It was always better to let these things roll off.

Before he could walk pass his car, the guy said, "Hey—"

Jason turned around.

"Do you know Jason Wylie?" he asked. "Have you seen him?"

Jason got a better look at him. He was an older man with short, thinning gray hair and rimless glasses. He was slightly taller than Jason with a potentially thick build under his tan windbreaker.

"I'm Jason Wylie. What do you want?"

"Oh, really!"

The guy came forward with his hand extended like he wanted to shake. Jason paused slowly to put his own hand out.

"My name is Fred Anston."

He gripped Jasons hand.

"I'm the father of you girl you put in a coma."

At the word *coma*, Fred pulled him close and landed a hard right into Jason's cheek. Jason tumbled back and Fred kept coming. Fred's fist fired like a nail gun into Jason's gut. A few more met Jason's face. Jason didn't even struggle. He figured he deserved it. Fred stopped as Jason collapsed to the ground, propped up on his shaky hands.

Fred Anston stepped back. "No hard feelings, kid," he said. "I know you didn't do it yourself. In fact, I'm a little grateful you killed that creep. Still, you are partially responsible for my baby being comatose."

He paused.

"The situation doesn't look good for her."

"I'm sorry," Jason said, wiping some dripping bile from his nose. "I really hope she gets better, Mr. Anston."

The man just nodded morosely and turned away. Jason scooped up his bag, woozily stood up and made his way up the stairs. What a day. What a life, so packed with thrills and spills.

Fumbling with his keys, he saw two of the unkempt burn-out kids from two doors down staring at him.

"Whoa, you okay, man?" one of them asked.

"Who was that?" asked another, leaning over the railing.

"You're bleeding pretty bad, dude. You're cut."

"I hope you enjoyed the show!" Jason replied, shoving himself inside. "I'll be here all week!"

He gently washed his face, made an ice pack and just soaked his numerous lumpy bruises. He couldn't remember being beaten up so badly; maybe in grade school when he had been a dorky freakish bully magnet.

More mental static. He couldn't think. He just wanted this crappy chain of events to work through their cycle and plop him out somewhere sane.

Eventually a knock came on his door, just when he was feeling better, while he was eating an eggroll and playing some music on his stereo. He knew who it was and wasn't thrilled to see her.

Sandra's jaw dropped when she saw his face and the front of his shirt. She asked him what happened.

"Obviously," he said, "I got my ass kicked."

"By who?"

"It was that girl's father. He wanted to deliver some sweet payback. No Serpenteras were involved, not directly anyway."

"I'm so sorry, honey."

She went into the kitchen for a fresh damp towel. She used it to clean away some places on his face he missed. She hopped back down to her apartment for some Tylenol, Neosporin and a proper face towel. Fred Anston had quite a thick class ring, a big one.

He was a grateful for her help. He certainly didn't have any medicine. Plus, the sympathy was nice. He didn't realize how much he needed some motherly attention. She dabbed his face, pouting in a mommy way, tussling his hair.

His stomach gurgled and he picked up his white bag from the floor.

Sandra quickly flipped the switch to business mode.

"I need to find those babies today. I held council with the Serpenteras. Big Mama is sorry and upset at what she did. She really just lashed out."

"Huh. Lashed out. Tell that to Fred Anston. I feel worse for him than for myself, even with this."

He held out the bloody face towel.

"I know. I know. I'm just saying there's nothing else to fear from her. We still need to act quickly. She's okay for now but . . . "

He groaned. "Right now?"

"Yep. We're going to the lair and do that psychic thing I mentioned."

A bigger groan, his chopsticks poised in the air.

"You can't weasel out of this. I know your luck is getting, well . . . "

"I'm eating! Can you stop yanking me around, please?"

"Well, eat then!"

He stood up. "I'm going to get you a plate and you're going to join me, then maybe we'll do your little psychic do-hickie down there."

"They are your *children*, you goof. Can't you pretend to care?"

"Are you sure this will even work? How about we try some normal ways? Like putting some ads in the paper or posting some signs around town."

She started to sneer. He was really just trying to lighten the mood with humor.

"Did you check the laundromat a few blocks away? Seriously."

"Actually, I did. Our Serpenteras like curling up in washing machines. It's really not an inborn instinct for all Serpenteras."

He chuckled. "How about Willie Chan's? They do like Chinese food."

"What? You're not funny. Just shut up."

"Seriously. They were weaned on this stuff. It's what I fed them."

She cast a thoughtful glance up, thinking. "You know . . . that kind of makes sense. Willie's is right through the woods from that house the car crashed into. A little bit of woods and a chain link fence would put them right behind Willie Chan's, where the garbage dumpster is."

She stared at him. "That's where they are. Has to be."

"I'm not such a dummy, now am I?" He plopped another chunk of chicken into his carton of rice and started mixing it around.

"Jason!" Her voice shot like a bullet.

"Give me that bag."

"What bag?"

"The white food bag near your feet. What's in it? Take it out!"

"Just sauce. Good ole funky Willie Chan's mystery sauce."

He tossed it up to her. She ripped it open. She popped the lid off the green sauce and screamed. The little container of sauce fell to the floor.

"*It's them*! It's *them*!"

"You're insane. That's it, Sandra. You are officially mentally unfit to be Serpentera den mother. You're fired. Pack up your desk and go home, babe."

"No no no . . . "

She started pacing the room.

"In the teacher's room at school! I saw the blue sauce sitting around. I could smell it all over that place. I thought it was just my imagination but . . . damn it, how could I have been so dense?"

"You need to take a mental siesta, Sandra, really. Try yoga, aromatherapy. Hey, how about pilates? Ever tried pilates? Suzanne Summers loves it!"

"That Bastard Chan. Charles. Fucking Bill Charles is his real name."

"Who? What?"

"The restaurant owner! Chan is not even his real name. He's not even Chinese. He's half Filipino, half Irish, the sleazebag. He's from a suburb somewhere in Connecticut. He tells everyone all about his real Chinese parents, a total bald-faced lie. Sheesh! He lies, he pays off health inspectors, greases politicians . . . he has lawsuits and sexual harassment claims that constantly swirl around him like flies. I know him. He's scum. He'd do whatever he could to earn a fast buck!"

"Next stop . . . Crazyville!"

She suddenly whacked the container out of his hand. Rice sprayed everywhere. He shouted.

"Stop eating that!"

He glared at her.

"Let's go! Get up!"

"You're insane."

"Let's pay him a visit, right now."

"Just what do you plan to do?"

She ran into the kitchen, her little mop of white hair swinging out. She came back holding his kitchen knife. "I'm gonna kill that scumbag!"

She ran outside the door. He ran after her. They jumped into her car. She huffed and threw up her hands. She had to get out and go back to get her purse. She didn't even have her car keys.

She was back in a flash.

As they were riding, he grabbed the knife out of her lap and threw it out the window.

"That's murder, Sandra! You don't know for certain if he did it. It's still just a hunch, a pretty far-fetched hunch at that."

"I'm part Serpentera, Jason. I know my kind when I smell them."

"Willie Chan's is packed right now. You're going to murder him on the busiest day of the week? Think!"

"No. I won't murder him right away. We'll just have a chat. I'll make him a bologna sandwich, then I'll kill him."

The golden rings in her eyes blazed, telling him she was serious.

***

The crowd at the restaurant had thinned out. She pushed her way to the front and demanded to speak to Mr. Chan. He wasn't there. The counter girl offered to summon a manager. Sandra said sure.

Jason took a good hard look at the poster on the wall that said, "Try Willie Chan's new Chow-Chow sauce!" He tried to stand front of it to block it from Sandra.

Willie Chan, or whatever his real name was, had a few other managers who looked after the place. They all were thin, swarthy, and vaguely Asian looking, like him. The one that emerged from the back asked them how he could assist. Sandra asked to see Mr. Chan.

"I'm sorry, ma'am. He's off today. May I assist you?"

"Well, yes. Sure. See, I work with Millman Promotions in Salt Lake City."

She felt around her pockets and glanced at her purse.

"Darn it, I don't have a card. Well, anyway, we spoke on the phone last week and I have some documents I need to drop off to him."

"I work pretty close with him and I haven't heard of . . . "

"Millman Marketing."

"But I can give you his email."

"Well, see, I'm on my way out of town. My flight leaves tonight. I can leave them here, but since I'm on my way to the airport . . . "

"He does spend a lot of time at the new store we're opening. But I can't guarantee you he's there right this minute."

"Fine. That'd be great. Where is it?"

"I'll give you the address. Hold on."

He felt around for a pen. Sandra's head bobbed hither and yon. She was struggling to keep herself under control. Jason was ready to restrain her. When the manager handed over the slip of paper, she bid him goodbye. Before leaving, she went around each table. Her face shuddered in horror.

"Pick those things up," she said to Jason, pointing to the sauce bowls. "We're taking them with us."

"Ummm."

He grabbed a few, cringing with embarrassment, mumbling apologies.

Heads shot up, angrily mumbling. The manager said, "Hey—"

Touching them gave him the heebie-jeebies, too. Hairs on his arms stood up. *They're your children.* In the little containers was Jason Wylie juice. Patrons of the establishment were feasting on an exotic extract of his loins, dipping eggrolls in his DNA.

*They were eating his children.*

At a small table by the wall, he saw The Magician gobbling on some of Willie Chan's finest. An open container of Chow-Chow sauce sat beside his meal, halfway empty. Another empty little cup was beside that one.

*He's having two of them!*

The tuxedoed fellow looked up and smiled at him with stuffed chipmunk cheeks. He waved.

*Dude, don't eat that shit.*

The maestro himself, fueling up on Chow-Chow power, ready to perform his amazing street acts.

Sandra pulled Jason by the elbow.

Outside, he quickly tossed the Chow-Chow sauces into a trash can.

She fired up the car, shaking. He could see her jaw muscles clenching. He offered to drive, even demanding at one point that she pull over and give him the wheel. She was weaving all over the lanes on the highway, cutting cars off, speeding up and slowing down. She passed the exit, then drove through the grass and dirt median to the other side.

They had to stop at two gas stations for directions to the street where the new restaurant was. It was serious exurban territory, some Atlanta satellite town Jason couldn't place. She still kept backtracking, making illegal U-turns, turning around, and shifting in and out of lanes.

At last they found a dusty looking building with the "Coming Soon: Willie Chan's Authentic Chinese Cuisine" sign. Some cars were parked there. Renovations were quickly underway.

Sandra parked miles from the curb, turned off the engine and said to him, "Take notes, sonny-boy. I'm going to show you what a half Serpentera old Jewish lady can do."

She ran around to the front of the restaurant and yanked at the front door. It was locked tight as a pillbox. She cupped her hands over the dark windows. There was nothing was going on in the front. Tables and chairs were stacked all over the dark future dining area. She trotted around to the back of the restaurant. He followed.

A large truck was back there. Banging and clanging came from behind and within it. A chubby Mexican guy with an orange hand truck stopped and gave them a sheepish stare.

"Excuse me . . . " she said to him.

He just stared, a toothpick dangling from his mouth.

"Habla Ingles?"

He shrugged. She put her hand on his forehead, gripped it tight, and leveled her eyes with him.

A flash of yellow sprang from her sockets.

Within seconds, his eyes rolled back and he slumped to the ground.

She headed to the open back door. Two other workers causally strode out. Lightning fast, she put her hand on one guy's forehead. The other guy shouted, "Dios Mio!" and tried to run, but a Bruce Lee-worthy maneuver tripped him up. Sandra merely flipped him over and it was nighty-night time for him.

A fourth guy came out. Jason felt obliged to help, so he wrapped his arms around the guy, pinning his flabby, sweaty shoulders so Sandra could give him the sleep treatment. "Buenos Noches, Pedro. " She dusted her hands in a joking manner and winked.

"Good lord, Sandra! You're gonna put me in prison. I'm officially on record for killing a guy. All I have is my crime free reputation! You're putting me in jeopardy."

"Would you like me to give you some quarters so you can go across the street and play video games?"

She cruised through, sniffing the air, and poking around the dark half-assembled kitchen. Parts of the stove were half off and sitting on a counter with some power tools. Lots of other parts in bubble wrap sat hither and yon. White boxes were stacked on the floor; some racks of cutlery were already being hung up and displayed. Jason looked into a dark freezer with the missing door; the metal shelves on the inside were clean, brand new and bare. Mr. Chan was sparing no expense.

"I don't think he's here."

Because of the lack of proper light and clutter, Jason didn't think she'd find the main office, if that was her goal. He was pretty sure she didn't have a concrete plan, expecting her to give up at any moment.

At least the Mexican dudes weren't hurt. Every day that passed by seemed to dangle another prison sentence; a nice orange jumpsuit, pressed, clean and waiting.

"We need to think this over before doing anything rash." Jason begged.

Guys like Mr. Chan were too busy to hang out in one place for too long. A successful guy like him probably already floored his Maserati to the golf course, leaving some lackey in charge of the little details.

Then, they heard a noise from further inside the building. Sandra had been heading in that direction, but started backing up. It was useless to explore further anyway. There was probably another hallway or two then nothing. Sandra probably didn't want to jump Willie in the dark. Even in the state she was in, Jason couldn't see her doing that. She hung back.

They heard voices down the hall chatting casually. Jason expected the more tinny voice to be Willie Chan. The conversation tapered off, and out strolled an older man with short brown hair and a thick push-broom mustache. He nodded to them as he casually cruised to the back door, fingers clutching a manila folder. He could have been anybody. Just some guy wearing a button down shirt tucked in his trousers.

His eyebrows furrowed when Sandra wouldn't let him pass. He started to speak. She grabbed his shoulders and beamed her gold lights into his eyes. He crumpled to the floor.

A voice called from the darkness, "You guys finished unloading that truck or what? Jose?"

The owner of the voice didn't show himself. He was

around the corner. The little hallway was lit up dimly. Jason got ready.

"Hey, Gus? Are you still there, man?"

The lights of the kitchen clicked on, a loud *twack* of a heavy duty switch. A thudding of footsteps.

"Lemme ask you something . . . "

There stood Mr. Chan, the only time Jason had ever seen him in casual garb, sans white chef uniform. He was wearing a sports coat with a vest underneath, trousers and a lavender scarf draped around his skinny neck. His head swiveled back and forth from Jason to Sandra, confused. He looked down and stared in shock at the floor.

"You killed my golf buddy!"

"No, I didn't. He's just sleeping. He'll be awake in a few hours."

Bewildered, Mr. Chan glared at her, "Who the fuck are you?"

A thick silence commenced, loaded with pure hatred provided by Sandra.

"You cooked my Serpenteras," she said. "*Our* Serpenteras."

"Serpent . . . what?"

Part of Chan's mouth hiked up in a smile, his little caterpillar mustache becoming animated under his nose.

"Oh, there's a name for those things?" He gave a huge toothy grin, the caterpillar elongating.

Sandra gritted her teeth, "Yes."

"I wouldn't know."

"Of course not."

"I just call them delicious! Sometimes I call them money." He threw up his white-gloved hands. "They're making Big Daddy richer by the day!"

He gushed mocking laughter. This was one of the few times Jason had heard him speak. Mr. Chan had come into the Book Barn a time or two, dressed like he was now, super-stylish. Jason had seen him at the restaurant in his white

Chinese cook uniform, his hands clasped together in front, bowing.

What a creepy charlatan. *He probably couldn't locate China on a map.*

Jason remembered those ridiculous low-budget commercials with Chan in full Chinese garb and the purposely garbled accent, "Come to Ri-lee Chan's! You'll riree like it!"

That stereotyped, racist, accent was gone now. He didn't even look Chinese in regular clothes.

Jason stepped closer to them, just in case he needed to jump in if something happened.

"I've been expecting someone like you would show up. Who do you work for, lady?"

"No one."

"Yeah, right. I don't believe a word out of your mouth. An average working man like myself catches a break, makes a little money and your people want to take it from me."

"Oh, that's rich."

"Your little creatures are cashed already, no evidence of the crime, so you don't have a case. Go on your way. Tell your people if they want to make something of it, they can speak to my lawyer. If those things are so hazardous, they shouldn't have escaped the lab, therefore they are just as guilty as me."

"I don't work for anybody. The Serpenteras weren't created by anybody."

"Like I care anyway. I don't want to know their life stories as long as they make that cash register ding."

"Oh! You are a disgusting human being, Mr. Chan, or Mr. *Charles*, you fake."

"Oh, c'mon. You know how the economy is. I have to stay in business, honey. When I find something people like, I give it to them. That's how capitalism works."

"Blah. You're wretched. Where did you find them? Eating from your trash? Then you decided to feed them to your customers? On a professional level, that's hideous enough."

"Aw, take everything out on the big bad businessman! Always with you types. You hippie nitwits couldn't turn out a dollar by your own efforts if you tried!"

Sandra started flexing her shoulders, her nostrils flaring. Jason prepared himself.

"It was an accident, by the way." Chan leaned in close to her, in a near provoking gesture. "Those little slimers were infesting my restaurant, every nook and cranny. Yeah, and the trash area, too! They could have put me out of business. You think I want to go out of business?

"I thought it was some kind of plot; someone deliberately sabotaging me. I got enemies. I stayed all night at my place hunting out every last one of those creatures. I put them in a big steel vat because I didn't know what else to do with them. Getting a reputation for having rats or roaches is dooming enough but *slugs* . . . "

"They're not slugs."

"So what? I don't care what you call them. Anyway, one of my staff heated up that vat thinking it was some kind of exotic new meat. She even tried it and told me how good it tasted. Then I tried it and added a few more spices. I waited until the next day to serve it. I wanted to be sure it was safe and that I wouldn't get sick. Instead of feeling sick, I felt powerful and surging with vitality."

He elbowed Jason and wiggled his eyebrows. "With the wife, and my assorted girlfriends, it's better than Viagra!"

Sandra looked ready to explode.

"People have been telling me all week how much energy and strength they are getting from my brilliant new Chow Chow sauce, seemingly like supernatural powers even."

"Maybe they wouldn't be so grateful if they knew the secret ingredient."

"Big deal. I'm helping people! You must be some kind of nutty animal rights person to not put the welfare of people over animals, especially bugs."

"Don't call them bugs!"

She shoved him. He stepped back, smiled and shrugged.

"They are sentient. They have their own language!"

"So, now you're the leader of the slug tribe. Wow, I'm impressed!"

Jason stepped in, told them to cool off. Miraculously, they abated.

Then Chan opened his stupid mouth again. "I was facing bankruptcy before those critters showed up. Now I'm in the black. I'm getting calls for interviews left and right and I'm featured in an article of Atlanta Food Journal next month!"

"I'm glad you're a celebrity now," she said, rolling up the sleeves of her blouse. "Those are the most interesting types to kill."

Mr. Chan's face stretched; his mouth opening in mock terror.

"Oh, don't kill me, baby! How about I write you a check and send you on your way? I'll pay you top dollar for more of those Serpent-whatsits. Name your price, sugar!"

She slammed him in the gut. He stumbled back against the doorless freezer opening, taking deep breaths. His face turned red, his mouth opening in to a rectangular grill of teeth.

"Nice uppercut for a little thing like yourself. Hoo! Oh, boy. I'm going to need a little medication, I think. I know just the thing."

He reached into his coat pocket and took out a small clear flask. Green fluid swished within it. He took a sip, smiled, then took another. Sandra started breathing heavy as she backed up.

"This is the last of it. I keep it for my own personal stash."

Jason asked, "I saw Chow-Chow sauce at the restaurant a little while ago. That wasn't the real thing?"

"There's a little left, but not enough to last through the day. This is all of it."

Chan raised the flask and gazed lovingly at it.

Taking it from his lips, he said, "I'm generous though. I share."

He spat it directly into Sandra's face. She fell back squealing and thrashing, with her hands clasped to her face, bluish green oozing through her fingers. A sharp elbow struck Jason's chest, shoving him backwards.

"C'mon, Big Boy! You want a piece?"

Jason gasped. Mr. Chan roundhouse kicked him into the sink.

The sneering restaurateur whipped a large hand gun from under his arm. He flashed it and turned it over in his hand. The monster handgun twinkled in the light. He shoved it into Jason's gut. Mr. Chan laughed at the ease of it all as he grabbed Jason's hair.

"Hey, lady! I'm going to splatter your grandson's brains all over this place if you don't get me more of those slug things."

Gun or no gun, being pulled by the hair was too painful just go along with. Jason reached up, grabbed Mr. Chan/Charles by the franks and beans and squeezed.

The skinny beast screamed in pain. The hand gripping Jason's hair loosened.

*Try to apply as much possible pain to this bastard.* Jason knew once he let go, the guy's Chow Chow superpowers would kick in and he wouldn't have this advantage again.

*They're your children.*

Jason squeezed harder, the old man screamed and the gun dropped. He could hear the sound of water gushing from the sink faucet. Sandra had made it to the sink and was frantically trying to wash the sauce off. She was still crying as she gurgled in the water.

Jason used his weight to try to slam Chan to the floor. With praying mantis-like agility, Mr. Chan's arms flew up and hooked themselves around the back of Jason's head, pressing hard; then he bent over and flipped Jason onto his back with painful force.

Chan screeched with laughter, placing his filthy shoe over Jason's mouth and nose.

"Lick it! Kiss it! Worship the shoe of the restaurant king of Atlanta! Ha ha ha!"

The leather sole of the wing-tipped shoe eased its way over to Jason's throat. Chan pressed down harder.

"Tell me where more of those things are. Tell me, you little punk! Maybe I'll let you live."

Just then, Sandra whipped around and charged.

Chan foiled her plan by springing backward onto the metal prep table. Sandra cursed him. She grabbed the first thing she could find, a wooden handled mop and pole-vaulted with it, feet forward, flying across the room. Chan quickly dodged her, causing her to rebound against the wall. But almost by magic, she stayed on her feet. She gripped a metal ladle on a rack of hooks near her and flung it, catching Chan in the stomach. He yelped. He hurled a set of salad tongs, which she knocked away with a quick forearm.

Jason was trying to find an angle to help her. Everything was going so fast. Cutlery flying, metal banging and clanging, fierce grunts; it was a wacko war zone. Sandra appeared to have a slight advantage. At most, Jason figured he would just get in the way.

Speaking of *in the way,* the golf buddy was under Jason's head. Gus. The fucker was snoring. As Jason started to sit up he felt lazy fingers drifting around his thighs. They didn't just drift; they had a purpose. They were going in deeper, headed for the gold.

"Ah, c'mon, baby," Gus said, drunk with sleep. "Give Gussy a lil' piece!"

He must have thought Jason was his wife or girlfriend. Jason threw the hairy hand off. Gus responded by farting. Using all the strength in his shoulders, Jason quickly shoved the molesting idiot into the doorless walk-in freezer. Partly in. The guy weighed a ton.

Jason crawled around, looking for the gun. He had a plan. End this ninja battle the easy way: Bang-bang. Problem solved.

He'd never fired a hand gun before and had an aversion to such a powerful object. But he could do it to in order to save Sandra. He'd prove to his daddy that he wasn't a sissy.

Pots were being thrown now and an equal number of grunts and shouts came from both sides. It was a tie so far.

*Why can't she hit him with the eye rays, like she did with the work crew? That was pretty darn effective.*

Chan did another skillful back-flip and landed squarely on top of him. Mr. Chan cried in victory. Jason's lungs seemed to shoot through his nose. He heard Sandra's sneakers whack onto the concrete floor.

Chan flipped around so he was right beside him, his knees shoving into his kidneys. Chan whacked him across the face then spun back into Sandra's direction, standing over both of them in a kung-fu stance, fists ready.

"Damn, girl, you are one fierce lil' mama!" spat the mustached villain, out of breath. "You keep coming and coming!"

"That's because I'm the real deal. Your super-juice doesn't last very long."

She chuckled as she watched him struggle to gain his balance.

"You are like all the others who think they can achieve power and strength through some quick formula. I spent over ten years arriving at my state, learning their language, going through the process with my Serpentera to slowly become one of them. You're a faker, a shyster and a laughable striver, Bill Charles! To gain real super powers takes hard work and commitment."

"I know more about hard work than you'll ever know!"

"True. You can run a business. You can do a payroll, manage employees, deal with banks and plenty of other worthwhile things."

She smiled. "But you can't kick my ass."

He reached into his coat pocket. As he took it out, he spun off the cap.

"This can though, right? Just enough left, honey. Oh, I *love* when you cringe like that!"

She was indeed backing away, eyes wide, muttering. Chan reveled in it, laughing.

"Okay, asshole. You've won."

"Really, I won?"

"Yep."

She bent down and picked up her purse. His eyes followed her.

"I brought something along as a bargaining chip," she explained. "I'll give this one to you. Just one! But after this one you have to promise you won't use anymore Serpenteras."

"It's in your purse? Open it!"

"Do you promise? Please?"

"Sure. Scouts honor! It'll make me enough money to get this branch up and running. That's all I need. No more Chow Chow sauce after that."

"Okay. I'll hold you to it."

She unzipped the small beige handbag and out flew Big Mama, in her little spindle form. Chan's greedy eyes followed Big Mama in awe. She floated over to the prep table. All the moisture pulled out of the air as she materialized in her full form, a sensation Jason had never noticed until now.

He hadn't seen Big Mama in this shape for a while. She flopped lazily across the counter, her little tail curling up; the eye bright and watchful.

"Oh, it's like a Christmas turkey," huffed Chan.

He crept over to it. He giggled, more than usual. His hands, formerly at his sides, disappeared to the front.

"You've made me so happy." He whipped around. "I don't need either of you anymore."

The bad man raised the big black gun and blasted Sandra, then Jason. The sound was like dynamite going off.

Chan didn't hit Jason and missed by a mile. Before he could fire the shot, Big Mama was already around his neck, her pointed tail entering his ear, going deeper. Bill Charles squealed in agony. Her huge tight body, now just an enormous throbbing muscle wrapped around his head.

She entered his ear and squeezed his head at the same time.

She did this quick, but not too quick, to ensure he suffer for his crimes. His screams were short but earnest. Jason turned away before he could wonder if the tail exited through the other side, catching the sight of blood gushing down Chan's neck and the eyes contorting into abnormal positions.

The hard floor and metal all around the room provided good amplification for the sounds of parts of Chan's head splattering.

She let go of the bastard and he fell.

Sandra was breathing heavy and groaning. She had been hit. The shock of all the gore had delayed Jason's response on checking on her. His mind was torn between the blood pooling around him from the dead entrepreneur and the wet darkness pooling across his friend's chest.

Not to mention that God-awful slaughterhouse smell.

"I'm dying, Jason. Please get . . . get me to the lair. Noooow . . ."

He stood and helped her to her feet, his shoes slipping.

*Do not look behind you, J-Man.*

The bullet hit her right above her left breast, dark blood saturating her light blue blouse under her coat. He moved quickly, the reality jolting him awake. He almost had to carry her. Her feet were useless, staggering and slumping out to the car. The work crew was still asleep. He laid her in the backseat.

He started to crank up the car when Sandra said, "Big Mama. Go get her."

"She can't come on her own?"

"Sh-she's sick, Jason. S-She's sad, sick and traumatized. She needs you. Don't. Don't worry about. About me. I still got a little . . . a little time."

"Are you positive?"

"Go."

He ran back inside. He avoided looking at the disgusting bloody body below. His feet slipped around in the wetness. That horrible meaty slaughterhouse stench assailed his senses again. He gagged and his stomach started to float.

Big Mama was on the table stretched out in her full form, all four feet of her. The striking sight of her helped him forget about the disgusting mess on the floor for a second.

As he approached her, she resumed her normal shape. He reached out and stroked her, her little tail looped warmly around his wrist and slid in between his fingers. He tried to not let his stomach hitch due to the wet warmness of it, the little yellow splotches...

He knew what it was.

After another stroke, she rose up and snaked around his waist. He headed out the door.

After opening the car door, Sandra said, "Don't come in yet. Stay out there. For one minute. H-hold. Hold her, Jason. Just one minute, okay? Please. After one minute. Then we'll go."

He did so. Big Mama slid around his shoulders. He stood out there for exactly one minute, stroking his warm snake woman.

A minute later, he bent to open the door. Big Mama miniaturized herself back into a little bright thread and flew into the backseat with Sandra. He cranked up the car.

"I really think I should take you to a hospital. The lair's too risky."

"I'll be . . . dead by then. If the doctors don't kill me, the bill will." She chuckled weakly.

"You need real medical attention. Look, I can't lose you. Big Mama is sick and Julia is brain dead. I've seen three corpses in the last few weeks. I can't let you die. We're going to a hospital."

"I'd be dead already if I wasn't half Serpentera. The

Serpenteras are the only ones who can . . . fix me up. Of course, I. Won't quite be the. Same . . . most likely."

"What do you mean?"

"Just take me to the lair."

He shook the steering wheel.

*Damn it! Why do I keep being put in these situations?* He shook his head in frustration.

"Okay, then. We'll go to that fucking cave."

# CHAPTER 10

HE PARKED ACROSS the street from the house zombie Carlos had crashed into. It seemed like ages ago. He could barely remember where it was, and his difficulty finding it was compounded by the pitch blackness that absorbed everything.

Luckily the Serpenteras knew where to go. A little worried dark blue squiggle started hovering around the windshield when they were half a mile away; Sandra's buddy. It flew into the car as soon as he opened the door swooping around with Big Mama in the back seat. Then it swarmed all around Jason as he charged out the door, buzzing around him like some annoying fly attracted to an open wound on his body.

He was able to ignore it and haul Sandra out. She had gotten cold and was shivering. He was almost afraid she had passed on. Time was running out.

The damn Serpenteras were panicking, too, and weren't much help in pulling her out of the back seat.

Whatever they did in the lair to charge up, they hadn't done it in a while, their glow dimmer in the blackness than it should have been. Spending too much time flying around the physical realm had drained them. Worrying about their human compatriots could also have been a factor.

Like with people, worry and stress sapped crucial energy.

*Great timing, guys.*

They snapped to attention once Sandra's stubby legs were out of the car. As he slipped his arm around her shoulder to very gently stand her up , knowing a hot bullet was inside her, the dark blue squiggly looped around her head and she was able to weakly stand on her own. She grunted in pain. She swore.

Sandra started muttering some of that weird language with her little Serpentera, sounding fairly alert, surprisingly so. Her tone in that freaky language sounded tough, thick, and to the point. She wasn't quite a death's door. She was bleeding badly, a lot of it on him. Her blouse and coat were soaked.

*I'd be dead already if I wasn't half Serpentera,* she had said.

True dat.

Standing at the old tire portal, the dark blue squiggly encircled Sandra's drooping head. Big Mama was doing the same to him. Jason felt himself stiffen, his body filling with that freaky near-paralysis. He was acutely aware of his insides tightening, something he didn't recall feeling before. His beleaguered stomach wasn't up to the task.

That sensation of falling, the mini-tornado, and the change in temperature was more like a Six Flags ride now, maybe due to the fact that he was anticipating it this time. Plus he wasn't running in a confused frenzied state with Big Mama helmet circling his head. Big Mama was less frenzied this time, as well.

He tried to help navigate Sandra down the rocky pathway, feeling blindly around, knowing it was no use, but attempting anyway. Big Mama around his head was a nuisance. She was over-staying her welcome.

*Give me back my eyes, damn you,* he wanted to say. *Turn back into that Glo-Stick thing and that's all I need.*

To complain would have been useless.

*Just a little light, no more dangling me around, shoving me this way and that. I've got legs and you don't, snakey, and I know how to use them.*

He couldn't see Sandra but knew she was back there. He felt a hand at his back, gripping his shirt.

*She needs me, see? I'm the important one. I'm her real friend. Sandra Millman wasted precious years of her life on you creatures, years she could have devoted to a normal life, a more fulfilling one with romance, travel, children, art, music, fancy parties, exotic foods...*

*Now this.* ***I*** *wouldn't get her shot. I'm the only real friend she has. I'm integral in this.*

Even though she was half Serpentera, she was still mostly human. Her Serpentera side was fairly recent. Most of her life was spent it as a human, with a life history mostly filled with human things: childhood memories, ice cream, walking to school, driving a car, riding a bike, sex, high school, college, weather, hobbies, cooking, working, reading, painting . . .

He suspected she had been married once. Surely she had some boyfriends. Lots of precious human memories there. Surely those things were still important to her.

Would she still have memories of all these things when she turned completely over to the Serpentera side? Most importantly, doesn't it matter to her?

Maybe she doesn't have a choice. Become a Serpentera or die.

What a choice.

That couldn't be the only option. They could use their magic to patch her up, put her in some kind of suspended state until she healed. He'd help! He'd bring her food and spoon feed her. He'd bring everything on a tray, a little glass of orange juice and a little flower in a vase, fluff the napkin out and hang it around her neck. It'd be a cute little napkin with kitty cats on it.

No matter how hard it would be to bring it down here, he'd do it with a big goofy smile on his face, enjoying every second.

*I'll quit work and look after her. No problemo. My gym bag stash will set me up for quite a while. I'll take over once they get her patched up. I'll be her devoted little man-nurse.*

A whole Christmas light show of Serpenteras surrounded her as they entered the cavern in a stunning wave of colors. He felt them, could see their blurry radiance beyond the Big Mama helmet.

She unfastened herself from his head and joined the laser show, mixed into it somewhere; somewhere his depleted vision couldn't detect. His body relaxed and felt better though, but tired and burned of energy. His hands and feet thudded around the slick, cool rock. He swore as he almost heaved face forward.

He remembered that abyss drop was somewhere, not too close, but out there. One couldn't be too careful. He remembered the spooks down in that creepy slit of a cavern; the cavern of the deep darkness.

*Don't stray too far.*

Even if he wanted to hurry the darkness, the overwhelming nothingness, would block him. His freedom was limited. He had to stay close to the Serpentera light show or else be frozen in place by the lack of sensory input.

They were busy at work on Sandra. Jason could only see her shoes for a while, as the brightly colored string army lifted her up and carried her into the largest cavern. This might have been the cavern he slept in eons ago, but his memory couldn't pinpoint. It didn't seem as high up as that one because he remembered climbing for quite some time.

He felt slighted by how quickly they whisked her away. No bit of consideration for him.

Despite how clingy Big Mama had been before, she appeared to have forgotten him now, just another squiggler in a sea of squigglies.

*Don't mind me. Be sure to call me again if you need a delivery service. Look me up. I'm in the phone book!*

He struggled to make his way up to the cavern, stumbling and sliding, and cursing them, his mutterings echoing in the crevices, reminding him how small he was to such a prehistoric wasteland of stony bigness. Rocks scraped across his knees and finger tips as he struggled, like crawling up some stone giant's tight stomach and pecks.

An up-slope of crags brought him to a standing position on a flat surface. Stumbling more, he hurried to the archway of the cavern. Feet. He saw feet. Her feet. He made out her scuffed Reeboks as they spun slowly in a gentle whirl of colors.

When they rotated her around he saw her head go limp, her eyes closed, and a fluff of short white hair falling over her face like a death veil.

He saw her mouth open like a yawn.

*She's still alive.*

The colorful Serpentera netting was more translucent than he first suspected and he could see her whole body as he leaned into the large cave. She looked very peaceful.

*But is it an 'I'm going to be okay' kind of peaceful or a nearing death kind of peaceful?*

The darkness and silence weren't hopeful or encouraging. She didn't look in the kind of shape where she'd soon be propped in a pleasant hospital bed with bouquets of flowers everywhere, little white cards in them signed by co-workers, and balloons with *Get Well Soon* floating above them.

Good ole happy normal stuff.

The somberness of the scene hinted at a huge oak casket with flowers around them and black dressed mourners with handkerchiefs bobbing.

There was still hope buried somewhere though. There had to be.

The brightest glow emanated from her left breast where the bullet had gone in. There was a pulsating blue spiral there. No doubt this was her Serpentera . . . performing surgery? The spiral eased into a light blue towards the center where apparently it was jiggling inside of her.

Her eyes widened, her facial muscles twitching, redness oozing across her face.

She was in pain, terrible pain. They were hurting her.

*Leave her alone! Don't hurt her. She's human! She's not one of you!*

*She needs a doctor, a medical staff, anesthesia, I.V. tubes, bleeping computer equipment.*

As if she had read his mind and sensed his concern, her head turned in his direction. He could see a sparkle of gold there, not quite like the gold rings she usually blazed. She was too weak to make the gold rings. They were normal human eyes. She looked at him placidly. He noticed a slight smile on her face.

*"Don't worry about me, you big goofball."*

He heard her, yet her lips weren't moving.

Her voice had been amplified by the stone walls, as clear as day.

Telepathy. Now telepathy.

Her eyes widened suddenly, bulging, with a look of such pain he had never witnessed before, as she turned ghost white. Then her eyes shut tightly. She gritted her teeth. The swarm of squiggly critters parted as a spirally red fireball with something bobbing in it, curved, then sailed out in a straight path like it was on a dire mission.

The bullet, they removed the bullet from her. And she was still alive. Incredible.

So he had misjudged their surgery capabilities.

The Serpenteras in the cave went about their work, even more diligently; the lively colorful net shimmered in more random directions, quicker as her head dangled outside of it. The cocoon around her had thickened.

Something looked different. He had been distracted following the bullet fireball. Yes, the big netting was becoming thicker, tightening around her, weaving around her, becoming brighter, and more intense.

With the bullet out, he expected the colors to fade away, to ease her down on the rock to rest, maybe stick some Serpentera IV tubes into her or whatever stuff they used.

They should be wrapping up the surgery process by now.

He had watched tons of surgeries on TV shows. Bandage her up and let her chill out.

Strands of hair stuck to her face. She appeared to be sweating. As cold as the cave was, she was sweating. His eyes watched in disbelief as colors began to knit around her neck. Why her neck? The bullet struck near her booby.

They were doing it wrong. They were going overboard.

He was tempted to intervene.

*Don't even think about covering up her face. I can put a stop to this if you do something dangerous.*

But the netting continued, up her neck, getting close to her chin.

*Everything should be fine now. Good job, team. We can go back and be regular neighbors again, Sandra and I. Look, she needs to get home and rest. She has to grade some papers. Work is going to pile up. Soon, maybe, we can hang out at her place and talk about art, and drink some wine, that fancy stuff she has in her wine rack. All in due time after I nurse her back to health. We can hang out and Big Mama can turn into her big cuddly self and curl up in my lap.*

*Can't we just be regular neighbors now?*

*I'll get a call from Melanie and she'll tell me Julia is recovering. Of course, I'll stay away for a while until she is back on her feet. Eventually we can resume our relationship where we left off.*

*Big Mama will understand. She'll come to grips with the reality that I'm a normal human male with natural desires for my own kind. I like hot long-legged blonds that giggle at my dorky jokes. I need a flesh and blood human in my bed, not some wispy shape-shifter.*

*Maybe I can have them both, my platonic Serpentera girlfriend and my real human girlfriend. It will all be so perfect. I deserve it anyway, don't I, after all this trouble and danger? Big Mama cares for me and wants me to be happy, so surely she will understand.*

*I just want things to be back to normal.*

The rings glowed powerfully from Sandra's eyes but the rest of her face went slack. It was like all the blood drained out of her face at once.

*She's dead. She just died. They didn't save her.*

His throat hitched, wetness dripping down his arms.

Her mouth was open but it didn't look like she opened it herself. She was utterly lifeless, a shell, the colorful cocoon enveloping her chin, holding it open. Before he could wonder *held it open for what,* a yellow stream of dust whooshed into her mouth like some kind of backwards smoke, scintillating in the slick reflective cavern walls; a powerful glow like fire without heat, undulating from a gold-yellow color to orange. Her eyes opened wide, very wide this time, and the gold rings in her eyes became round fires, then bright yellow spotlights.

He tore away from the sight, feeling stricken, and slid down the smooth rock doorway of the cavern, his senses fading. His brain quickly recovered, and he blindly attempted to regain his feet, bathed in the wetness of tears and disorientation. When his vision cleared, he fixed his eyes on her again.

He had to situate himself at just the right angle to watch it. Even the physical appearance of Sandra Millman was fading.

She had the gold-socketed eyes of a malevolent space creature.

*Who or **what** are you now?*

Whether she was dead or just transforming into some other form, it was all the same to him. Someone else he cared about was going away. Someone else was leaving him. Like all the rest, like his parents had when he was eighteen. *It's time to fly the coop, son,* his dad had told him one day, *you got to get a job and take care of yourself from here on out.*

Big Daddy tried to convince him to join the military, pushing the Air Force because of his consistent B average in high school. At least his dad cared enough to suggest things.

His mother didn't say squat. She was distracted by her new dumb-as-a-sack-of-hammers boyfriend, the second half of her life that didn't concern him.

His parents fled to their respective recliners, sofas and TV shows and lovers. Their parenting days ended when he turned that magic age of eighteen.

Then Jill and Julia left him. His high school friends went bye-bye fast. Dave and Chris would be next. It was only a matter of time.

*Jason, listen to me!*

Sandra.

There she goes again. That telepathy.

*This might be the last time I can converse with you like this.*

Okay.

He crept over.

*I'm okay . . . really . . .*

Her disembodied voice was already breaking up.

*Take care of Big Mama.*

He noticed her face turning color, slowly brightening into a light orange color. Her cute little triangle of a nose started melting away. It simply flattened then was gone. Her white hair dripped and fell away like a wig, nothing more.

Those wide eyes blazed.

Not dead eyes.

*Alive.* More alive than he could ever comprehend.

Slowly her lights were merging from two blazing eyes to one. One-eyed like the rest of them.

Her brethren.

Her mouth sealed up, the wavy color cocoon spinning faster over it. Her ears were long gone too. All the organs and bones so lovingly given to her at birth were being discarded, chucked aside like worn-out parts, useless matter, outdated components, *garbage, refuse, blah blah blah, can't use that lowly human gunk anymore, Sandy of the Serpenteras! We have been using you all along to create this beast, our armies of drones mindlessly guiding you to this point, this point where we converge into a new species, so useful you were and how useful for our purposes you will be as we spread throughout the planet and create more like yourself . . .*

There was no point in thinking of it as a *her* anymore, *it* was merely a smooth fiery orange thing beaming two holes of brilliant light, soon to be cinched up in orange. A long orange snake born of color and flames.

For what reason? Is there one? Maybe just to exist?

Was existence that big of a deal?

Surely not here in this cold place, this God-forsaken sepulcher not worthy of any other life forms besides these basic looking snake critters.

Tendril critters hovered above and around the transforming thing, excitedly. They looked happy.

The bone of her skull began to liquefy, undulate, all orange, gold and yellow. The show was over, just a few last minute wrap-ups, probably compacting her body into a smaller size; certainly painful if she had a human body.

Some crazed alien language started sputtering in his head. She was still trying to talk to him, perhaps trying to let him know the transformation had succeeded. He assumed it was her anyway. It was fading. It didn't last long.

It felt Satanic, not right. It was *at the very least* cruel. He turned away and just started walking in the direction he assumed was the right way, stumbling.

*Fuck it. I might as well fall into that abyss hole with my pocket change.*

Big Mama finally turned up, extricating herself from the colorful wave and wrapped herself around his shoulders, her warm snake body forming. She wrapped herself around him for no particular reason. It was obviously a hug.

He started walking. He felt along the walls, utilizing his legs while he was allowed to. Big Mama unfastened herself from his shoulders, going up towards his head in a slightly confused manner. He just kept walking. He wanted out.

There was nothing left to contemplate or discuss. Theater lights were coming on. The show was over.

He endured the next part, passing through the portal, like a brave little soldier, just letting her do what she had to do, relieved just to be going.

Emerging back into the outside world, he fell to the ground and took his time standing up. Big Mama floated in the darkening dusk. He felt like they were saying goodbye. It was the end.

He had no more connection to these things. He had done his job and fulfilled his duty like a good little minion, like the serpents wanted. He had been a good little boy to them, a useful object; a seed provider to the grand scheme.

She just hovered there.

*How am I going to understand them without Sandra?*

He didn't know what else to do.

*What do you want? Can't I just clock out and go home now? I'm bushed.*

Maybe she wanted to tell him something, console him in some way. Make sure everything was cool between them. He thought about giving her the A-OK symbol but that would seem phony. Finally he decided to blow her a kiss.

That's what he did, although it felt meaningless.

***

He kept his eye out for a little orange Serpentera to stop by his place, do something goofy, play a joke on him, like slide up behind his pants and give him an underwear wedgie.

That would be her style. He would welcome it.

*She's probably learning the ropes.*

Transmogrification had to take longer than a few hours, days or even weeks. He knew he'd just have to be patient.

As weeks crossed over into the next month, Mike Shibble stopped by to ask Jason if he had seen her. Of course, Jason knew why Mike was looking for her. She owed him rent and she was his de facto manager of the place. He didn't seem the least bit concerned with her wellbeing.

Just business and money, money, money. You know the deal. That's all that matters anyway.

That little blue truck, all loaded with ladders and paint cans, told him that driving all the way out here to locate his oddest tenant was just wasting precious daylight for him.

Jason just played dumb, said he had no clue.

Morosely, he wondered what to do with her stuff. He just left it all down there, in the cavern. Most of her stuff was too girly for him plus it would have been disrespectful to raid her place.

He did take her paintings. These were special. He hung them up on his wall.

The couch was special too. Because it was so damn comfortable. And brown leather.

She'd want him to have it.

Good ole Sandra Millman. She's basically immortal now, anyway. As long as she charged up in whatever doohickey they charged up with in the cavern, she could look forward to a beautiful peaceful existence devoid of death.

No strife, no traffic, no work bullshit, no disease, no root canals, no insurance companies, no clogged toilets, no hassle from the wicked world at all.

*She made it.*

Mr. Shibble didn't waste much time cleaning her place out, as if he relished the opportunity. Jason saw a truck pull up one morning and by the time he came home from work that day, her apartment was empty, the door was hanging open.

All of her stuff gone. Sandra was gone.

Not a spirit now but dead, snuffed out like a flame. Depression sunk its fangs into Jason deeply now, swallowing him up like a python on a mouse.

Jason's Pabst consumption increased as the weeks went by. He blew off the Turban more, preferring the solitude of his apartment.

*Why have friends anyway? They just move on and leave you . . .*

One night, while he was feasting on his sudsy liquid dinner, the can suddenly upended into his lap. A little fiery orange tendril gripped the frosty end of it.

Coldness gushed onto his lap.

"Oh, you dirty little—!"

So very sneaky! She whizzed around his head and made his hair stand up. He was sitting on the floor with his boom-box stereo as usual. He covered his head in a kind of duck-and-cover motion until she flew off of him.

The wispy orange Sandra creature hovered in the air like a flying worm of fire, pulsing with vitality. It thickened and blew itself up like a balloon. Within seconds the disembodied head of his ex-neighbor hung above him, little oval glasses and helmet of white hair.

"Well, hello, neighbor!"

*Now, this is different.*

"So . . . " he said to the hovering face. "You're the Great and Powerful Oz now?

He chunked his now empty beer can into the face and watched her splinter into nothingness. It was worth it to see the look on her wall-sized face.

Her features took a long minute to re-knit into the air. Lines and colors shifted and re-shifted frantically. When it was complete it looked none too happy.

"Don't do that, doofus!" she bellowed. "It's taking every atom I have to do this."

"I'm surprised you still have atoms."

"Oh, I got atoms to spare, buddy-boy. I'll put some of these *atoms upside* your head next time you do that!"

"I'm sorry. It's really good to see you. So can you pop in on me like this a lot?"

"No."

"It's like that fear, you know, that your dead relatives can see you in, um, intimate moments."

"Ew. Just, so very, *ew*. If I had hands, I would shove my fingers down my throat to induce vomiting. What an image."

"Well, I didn't mean necessarily that . . . "

"I just now obtained this ability. You think I'm going to hide around your trashy apartment and spy on you? You wish. I have better things to do than watch you chugging beers, reading, sitting on the toilet, Q-tipping your ears . . . "

"My finest moments, actually."

Her lips were still moving but no sound was coming out. Her huge face was dimming as if her battery was giving out. It returned suddenly, full force.

"Oopsy, Jason. Fading out. Look, take care of Big Mama. She's complaining that you're ignoring her."

"Want me to take her to the movies? Go roller skating? Hey, tell ya what. I'll talk to my travel agent about booking a romantic *Caribbean cruise*. It's a bit off-season now but..."

Her enormous eyes rolled to the ceiling.

"She's no Christy Brinkley but at least you have someone that cares about you. Yeah, I do spy on you and see you sitting there every night guzzling beers, reading those cheesy graphic novels. Even your literary tastes have hit bottom."

"They are not cheesy."

"Oh, yes they are. Please stop torturing yourself about Julia. You're in a rut, kid. Seriously, for God's sake, get a life."

"Me? Get a life? At least I'm not some disembodied head hovering arou—"

Poof. Her face popped like a bubble.

He waited. She didn't return.

*Disappearing before I get a chance to insult you back? Some friend you are.*

He felt like an idiot for missing her like he had. All that grief and she shows up just long enough to criticize him.

He waited and waited for her to show up again. At least to get in a dig to retaliate for her "Get a life" remark.

He could go to the caverns and do it if he was so inclined. But he wouldn't.

That would have to involve Big Mama.

***

She hung out with him a few times a week. She enjoyed Sandra's couch.

*I'm sure you spent a lot of time on this thing with Sandra, sitting there with a box of tissues, complaining about what a lousy boyfriend I was.*

It got to the point that it seemed Big M liked snuggling with the couch more than him, going underneath it, snaking through the cushions and pillows, always knocking them off, which was annoying.

He never knew when she would make an appearance. She just popped by when it was convenient. He knew the real purpose, or was suspicious of it at least.

One night he awoke to see his elementary school teacher, Mrs. Morgan, in fishnet stockings and a tiny bra with red tassels.

And a can of Reddi-Whip. Always with the Reddi-Whip.

*How kinky does she think I am?*

She should have known this form wouldn't work again.

Hovering over his bed she transformed many different pleasing forms: Cameron Diaz, Bettie Page, Eliza Dushku, the chick from the underwear ad he kept in his drawer . . .

Now that he was wise to the methods of the succubus, he didn't get fooled by these visions. They hovered in his doorway like eight millimeter film projections, a more colorized version of the Screamers, than actual flesh-and-blood women.

*Nice try, snakey. I'm onto this.*

He slept with the doors locked and his pants on tight.

# CHAPTER 11

ALL THE BABY squigglies flew away. Where they were headed, what they would do, he could only guess.

Let nature deal with them.

Julia never recovered and remained insensate in her hospital bed, a hospital he was afraid to visit, afraid he wouldn't be welcome.

He had given up hope. Melanie kept him informed.

Bubbly Melanie finally quit the Book Barn because of the lack of hours. Part-timers were always the first to get squeezed. He heard she got a job a Beecher's and was still going to school.

He never got his promotion. It was like the subject was just dropped. Through the grapevine, he'd heard some falling out between Janet and the other managers. Lori Driscoll, the store manager, remained a flaky, quirky, annoying tyrant. He could tell his handling of the Roger incident never really impressed her anyway. He was just another drone sucking off the payroll.

They replaced Roger's position with someone from the outside, some ex-Walmart manager with no-nonsense retail experience and scant knowledge of literature.

That wasn't a prerequisite anyway. The dumber the better seemed to be their preference. Good ole Book Barn.

This manager, Dorothy, didn't like him too much. She didn't dislike him either. She was neither unfriendly nor friendly, just neutral. In typical fashion, she quietly ordered him around like all the others, more quickly to point out the slightest mistake than to even hint at a compliment.

What a system.

Willie Chan's was taken over by Chan's brother, the guy they saw at the restaurant that morning. The new location was never opened.

Jason was just relieved to have not been linked to Chan's death. He saw some police checking out Sandra's car one day, not long after that incident. They knocked on her door and lingered around a few minutes. That was all. The police left.

The restaurant suffered because of Willie's demise.

The public's enthusiasm for it petered out, returning Willie Chan's to its former mediocre status.

Its brief Chow Chow limelight was snuffed out.

It wasn't as if he knew this first hand. He concluded this from driving by it to and from work, a crumpled Taco Bell bag in his passenger seat now.

No more Willie Chan's.

He stopped calling Jill. It was time to let that die. Cut the cord. Set her free.

Maybe he'd call her in a few months. When he got internet, which he was planning to do, he would friend up with her on Facebook or something.

He could keep the pretend interest in her life going with that.

Woo hoo.

Then Dave hit him with a whammy.

He was moving away, far away. It was bad enough that Chris had coupled up with a chick and was showing up less and less at the Urban Turban. Hell, even Lotus quit the Turban.

Lotus, for God's sake.

At the point when Jason was most acutely aware of his growing isolation, Dave had to inform him, over a cool can of Pabst, that he was moving to Miami, Florida.

Dave's brother was going to hook him up with a shift manager job at a factory there.

"Dude, *a salary*. I thought I'd never obtain such a state."

"I'm stoked for you. A salary. Wow."

Quietly, Jason was dying inside. It was apparent at this point Fate had it in for him; that the universe itself plotting daily to create inventive ways revel in his misery.

The same ole pattern, that evil, twisted, maddeningly asshole-ish pattern, give just enough good things to him, then rip them away. All good things in his life, especially friends, eventually turned on him.

*Everyone is moving on except you, loser. How's that manager position working out?*

Dave filled Jason in on some more hopeful details about how awesome Miami was going to be, all the improvements it had over Atlanta.

"Imagine living so close to the shore. I've heard great things about South Beach. It's like L.A. or something. And the Everglades. They are swamps, right?"

"Alligator infested swamps, yes, indeed."

"You'd like Miami. Lots of famous writers scribble about that place, some of your favorites."

"Yep. Charles Willeford, Carl Hiaasen, John McDonald . . ."

"You're welcome to tag along, J-Man. Maybe my brother can hook you up with something too. I can't guarantee anything. Hell, a job is a job. We're still young. You could probably use a change, too."

"So, what are you trying to say? For your information, I'm proud of the prolonged state of rigor mortis that is my life."

Even though he said it joking, he meant it. He just shrugged and tried to change the subject.

Leaving was impossible. He couldn't leave. Big Mama would hunt him down and kill him.

*No, she wouldn't.*

She couldn't kill him with Carlos holding a board over his head in her most enraged state, so if he fled town, it was possible she would get over it. Despite how difficult, even impossible, it was to discern her feelings, at her core, he knew she cared about him and wanted what was best for him.

It still seemed impossible, risky.

Just leave? No way.

He couldn't take her and the whole extra-dimensional lair with him. There was only so far she could travel.

People talk about relationships "weighing you down". He had a whole cavernous netherworld tied to his ankles.

The *Get a life* remark still stung. Sandra had planted a seed of an idea in him. Maybe that's why she never reappeared. So that little dig would incite some action out of him.

*Well, it worked.*

He basically made up his mind right then, at the Urban Turban with Dave. His mind was made up from the word Go.

He went. His current life was dead anyway.

Everything was fair and square. He broke his lease, handing over an extra month's rent to Mike Shibble. He even checked with the police department to make sure they wouldn't be suspicious and alert the FBI, or whatever they did.

Sergeant Darrow, a pretty nice guy, let him know that he was in the clear.

"Enjoy your youth, kid. You've got nothing to worry about here."

He was free.

He kept remembering Sandra melting into that Serpentera thing and had nightmares about it even. In the back of his mind, he was afraid Big Mama would turn him into something like that. Maybe he'd meet a girl and Big Mama would turn her into something like that out of spite, some slick faceless creature, sucked into a world that was still mysterious, even to him.

Sandra would bitch him out for leaving like he did.

He did feel ashamed.

But he had to go.

As he was pulling away from his apartment, all of his belongings packed in his car, a young version of Kathleen Turner, ghostly and two dimensional, wearing a revealing night gown and garter belts, waved him good-bye with a handkerchief.

He saw her vanish into a squiggly line and fly away.

# CHAPTER 12

JASON GOT A job as a bartender in a fairly upscale place, a place with chandeliers, polished oak, and an in-house jazz pianist. Celebrities came in often. The owner and head chef smoked doobies on the back patio after closing.

Jason started out as a dishwasher, then a bar back. The staff liked him, so they trained him as a bartender. It wasn't his dream job, but he got to meet interesting people and the pay was nice. The pay was a lot better than retail and the hours were more stable.

Dave moved out after a few months to live with his new girlfriend. Jason had the whole place to himself. It was scary at first, but he got used to it.

Dave was awesome. He was the Anti-Carlos as a roommate, the best roommate ever. He was still much better with women.

Jason had met a few women at his job but preferred to stay single. He had a brief physical relationship with the flaky hostess, but that was all it was.

Dave was careful discussing this subject with him. He knew Jason was still wounded from the Julia incident. Dave was always reminding him, "It's not your fault what happened". "You're a good guy, Jason. You didn't mean it to happen".

Dave was pretty quick to pick up on Jason's somberness

while they were roommates and, as good friends do, wanted to get to the root of it.

Jason would never get over Julia. She had been a smart upwardly mobile young woman tragically cut down in her prime, in a hospital hooked up to machines to live.

Because of him.

It was impossible to forget.

He'd just have to live with it. Like Sandra, Big Mama, and Jill, Julia was another ghost of his previous life.

She was the spookiest ghost but a ghost, like the others, who had to stay in the cavern.

She had to remain in the cave of the deep darkness.

One humid Miami night, he got a knock on his door.

He wasn't used to knocks on his apartment door, especially at night. Miami was still a dangerous town in his mind; gangsters and cocaine cowboys lurking around every corner.

There was lots of crime, more than Atlanta. The knock was urgent but gentle sounding, so he opened it.

The ghost was there. She was real though, flesh and blood.

He stood mouth agape, muted with disbelief.

A weak headlight glow emanated from behind her; where she had driven the car, whose ever it was, across the lawn, through some bushes, and almost into his door.

She was smiling widely, wearing a filthy, and ripped hospital gown. Her hair was all over the place, long and unwashed with some leaves, dirt, and a trash in it. She wore no shoes.

Within seconds, her hands went around his waist, around his neck, over his shoulders, feeling him all over like she wasn't used to having arms.

She wasn't used to touching things with hands.

Especially him.

She shot forward and lunged a very awkward kiss at him. Her nose plowed into his. It was a very bad kiss. He saw that her arms and her hands were shaking, vibrating. This seemed familiar.

She was quite animated for a recently awakened coma patient who had driven thousands of miles in a stolen car.

"Julia?"

She just grinned, a big toothy grin.

"Julia? Is that you?"

She shrugged.

"Are you all right? You look—"

Her retinas suddenly glazed over in gold.

Not rings but blazing headlights.

Normally, they would have knocked him out. Now it felt like an electrical jolt, creating the opposite effect.

He knew now and was damned if he could figure out how she did it. His first thought was how much of it was Julia and how much of it . . . wasn't.

The glowing eyes were actually very . . . *sexy*. Her chest looked considerably bigger; little Serpentera enhancement?

*Congrats, Serpy-girl. You discovered a form I can't resist. And she's also real.*

He repeated his question, "Are you all right?"

To answer his question, she gave him the hand symbol, the thumb and the index finger in a circle.

A-Okay.

www.ingramcontent.com/pod-product-compliance
Lightning Source LLC
Chambersburg PA
CBHW051956220626
47052CB00004B/969

* 9 7 8 9 1 9 7 9 7 2 5 3 6 *